MYSTERY STORY

MYSTERY STORY

David Pirie

FREDERICK MULLER LIMITED
LONDON

First published in Great Britain 1980
by Frederick Muller Limited, London, NW2 6LE

Copyright © David Pirie 1980

British Library Cataloguing in Publication Data
Pirie, David
 Mystery story.
 I. Title
 823'.9'1F   PR6066.I/
 ISBN 0–584–31103–6

Printed in Great Britain by Biddles Ltd., Guildford.

For K.G. wherever

'Our subject, then, is mystery, a quality so important to sexual excitement that the two are almost synonymous.'
Dr. Robert Stoller: *Perversion, the Erotic Form of Hatred*

'Suppose that the development of male human sexuality has gone awry, that a wrong turn has been taken. We must, then, accept the possibility that it may be changing for the worse.'
Dr. Max Byrd: *The Dream and the Desire*

*Somewhere at least two streets away, Jane heard the screech of tyres –
then stillness. It was quiet and bitingly cold for an October night.
Little clusters of leaves formed a chequered pattern around her feet. She
wished Jo was with her. Only her ridiculous heels scraping on the
pavement. Clicking and scraping.*

*They were odd, she thought looking down at the shoes, trying to
distract herself from a sudden inexplicable pang of fear. The whole
rig-out was archaic and invariable. But in a way she still enjoyed its
stupid arbitrary power: from the arched heels to the scooped blouse and
tortured make-up. Which quirk of psychological evolution, she wondered, had dictated these as come-ons? Yet their very impersonality
helped to clarify her mission. A combat uniform. She stamped mentally
on her own highly developed sense of melodrama.*

*For whenever she managed to get someone with her here in the town,
it did seem like winning a battle in a war. Every time she saw their
staring tumescent male eyes above hers, she felt those eyes could never
look quite the same again. Other changes could come from that one
change.*

*Looking down the empty street and quickening her pace slightly past
a darkened Marks and Spencers, she wondered why there had been so
few in the hotel tonight. And why was it so silent? Things had been
going well, but now this quiet was like a hush before battle. She should
have changed back in the hotel, then she could move faster. But the
transition would have been too obvious.*

*She thought she heard a sound from a lane on the right. She stopped.
Then gently hitched up her skirt. If one of them was waiting he would
want to see that. Her body had to remain the impersonal entity that
drew curiosity.*

*No-one appeared, and she turned into the street that would take her
back.*

*Unexpectedly an engine fired into life and two lights turned the
corner. Jane was momentarily scared and then as the large car drew
closer, she smiled in scornful recognition. If only she could work on*

them, everything would be a lot simpler. On an impulse she switched into her familiar role, pausing with a leg forward in the headlight glare. In that moment for the hundredth time she reflected on the miserable irony that the day she was raped on the streets of this town would be a kind of victory. Even if she was not around to celebrate it afterwards. As the door opened, she prepared the pitch and accent of her voice. A man got out and looked at her. Two others followed him.

'I didn't do well tonight,' she said, steeling herself, 'so you people can have credit.'

They smiled but was there something tight about the eyes she didn't like? Her part had a life of its own.

'How about the car?' she said. 'It's big enough.'

One of them – thin and long-faced – came up close and put a paternal hand on her shoulder to escort her to the car but, as they walked, the hand soon quivered and dipped until it was moving jerkily over her behind. She felt a flush of triumph. This had to be the climax.

Then she was in the black car, sprawled on the back seat, as hands fumbled with buttons and zips. She could hardly wait to see the whites of their eyes. Her only regret was that no-one else was going to witness this. The street was still deserted.

'How do you fancy it first?' she said, wanting the effect of directness. And then realising, stupidly, that none of them had yet spoken.

They still stared at her mindlessly.

'We'll decide 'ow,' said one. And suddenly for the first time she felt a proper fear. His accent was not local.

In this moment a series of terrible truths flooded her mind. With a convulsive naked movement she lunged for the door. But already their hands were on her. And she was utterly pinned down on the seat. As the first one gripped her tightly by the throat and moved to enter, Jane felt the pure self-contempt of someone who has unwittingly devised and orchestrated her own death.

And she knew there was no victory.

PART ONE

ATTRACTION

Chapter One

From the beginning there was always something odd about that Christmas. Most of London's meagre decorations had blown down in a series of freak storms and the city looked grimmer and seedier than I'd ever seen it. There had been a few terrorist bombs but the atmosphere wasn't so much paranoid as exhausted. After the emergency coalition government had dug in its heels and mopped up most of the pockets of racial disturbance, a numbness seemed to descend on England. I had treated myself to a full tank of petrol, but as I drove past Trafalgar Square late on Christmas Eve, even the pigeons looked like mechanical toys from a past that could be scarcely remembered, far less recreated.

Things were made worse by the fact that I'd somehow persuaded myself to stay in the city over Christmas.

For the past ten years – after voluntarily abandoning medical school and a short, hateful stint in the promotions department of a record company – I had been making a reasonable career out of non-fiction books and psychologically inclined journalism. A study of the romantic lives of various leading nineteenth-century spies had sold well, as had a long illustrated account of the English punk summer of 1977 and its musical offshoots, and a speculative history of the effects of drugs on human personality. I enjoyed these assignments and through them I was able to do some other books, less obviously commercial, including a biography of the Belgian fantasy writer, Jean Ray. In spite of all the upheavals in the social climate it had even been a happy time. London was still a pleasant place to live if you were young enough to enjoy it and, until a few months earlier, I had been with Karen.

Then she made up her mind to go off to Finland for a year to teach and, almost as a challenge to my own potential loneliness, I had decided to attempt a working Christmas. For some time I had been trying to finish an ambitious book

3

about current sexual research and, after receiving a fairly hefty advance, I was now determined to get it written, even if it meant a lonely period in my London flat. And that was how the whole thing began.

On Christmas Eve I had attended a party overrun by lonely media people trying to drown the idea of Christmas. It proved so drunken and depressing that I ended up in somebody's flat, making an unsuccessful attempt to phone Karen in Finland. The first of a series of bad connections.

So I woke up on Christmas morning feeling distinctly alone. And the unspoken fact of Christmas made it worse. I reflected on that as I sat on the edge of the bath, trying to filter a sense of reality through a residue of sexual and violent dreams. Christmases, birthdays, anniversaries – all potentially grim occasions – but they served to disguise what was grimmer. And that was the passing of time and old age and loss. Celebration was an ingenious distraction, a masque.

It was because I needed some kind of distraction that I switched on the radio as I got into the bath. And you could say it was because I switched on the radio that the whole thing began. Perhaps on rare occasions, a tiny fact like that can change the whole direction of your life or even cause your death. Sometimes I wonder what would have happened if the radio and the telephone hadn't been working. Or if Karen had still been there to spend Christmas: waking up late, jokey presents, then a walk in the frost on the heath before getting pleasantly drunk in the evening. But I switched on the radio.

I wasn't listening to it too closely at first. A pop record had something about 'Your pa should see you hangin' with a rope around your neck'. There were a couple of songs like that. Sick records were vaguely in fashion again that winter.

The music tied in well with the news. One of the northern white defence leagues had hit a black carol service in Bradford, leaving behind scores of bodies. Power blackouts were expected over parts of Scotland. Then there was a more traditional missing persons item from the Midlands, which seemed oddly old-fashioned set against the rest of the news.

'Police in Weston, Staffordshire. . .' droned the newsreader in an irritating monotone which could have signalled anything from a missing monkey to the annihilation of a small community.

4

The name Weston stirred forgotten and dangerous associations before a second name jolted me upright.

'. . . are searching for 32-year-old Johanna Parver whose clothing and personal belongings were found by a roadside a few miles from the town in the early hours of the morning. A spokesman for the Staffordshire police said the case is being provisionally treated as a murder enquiry.'

The emotion that that dry formula aroused in me was hard to control. My mind raced back to a summer in the late sixties and in particular to a phone-call. Anyone who's experienced a conversation with an overdose victim knows the feeling. It's like trying to hold onto a fistful of water as their tenuous hold on reality falters and slides. And a phone-call like that had been my last connection with Johanna Parver. Nor was there any mistaking the name: I could still hear her mother's dry announcement that there was not a single Parver in the London telephone directory because it was among the rarest names in the country.

Sometimes the more intense a relationship, the more likely it is to disintegrate while still alive, like a victim of leprosy. As soon as her stomach had been pumped, she was rushed to America by a mother who divided men unequally into brutes and heroes. But in all the years since I could never completely forget Johanna. She was like a ghost who occasionally looked over my shoulder at the feast.

Somehow you don't expect the radio to thrust past phantoms at you while you're in the bath. I felt like I'd been temporarily reunited with the dead.

A tangled network of emotion stayed with me as I dressed. I kept trying not to visualise the pile of clothes in a heap beside the road. I wondered if I should phone someone up, but I couldn't think of anyone to phone. The previous day I had been struggling with a chapter on rape and now the jungle of statistics and medical reports on my desk, filled me with revulsion.

I was staring out of the window, trying to force myself to begin work when the telephone started ringing. Continuously. The old interrupted ring had been replaced some years earlier by a jarring continuous bell. The GPO claimed it was more efficient but plenty of people suspected that there were other, more sinister, motives behind the switch. The government was constantly increasing its powers of surveillance. Many people had given up their phone in protest.

There was a long silence at the end of the line before a polite male voice said my name.

'Yes' I said.

'We're trying to locate someone I believe you know. Johanna Parver.'

For a moment I thought I'd misheard him. Johanna had not been part of my conversational world since the sixties. Now within the space of two minutes I had heard her name twice. No-one, outside of my closest friends, could possibly have been aware of our relationship.

'Can I ask who this is?'

'Yes Sir. This is Whitaker, we're investigating the case from Weston.'

'I haven't seen her for at least ten years. But how did you know about me?'.

'That's not important,' he said in the same friendly tone. 'Thank you for your help.'

The line went dead.

I stood with the phone in my hand, still in a state of bewilderment, and then rang the Scotland Yard switchboard, asking for the number of the Staffordshire investigation team. The good-natured sergeant who was handling public enquiries in Weston confirmed after a brief delay that Whitaker was working with the special CURV unit, but they were not taking calls at present. I couldn't think what CURV meant.

'The Commission,' he explained. 'They were called in after the Triar business last October.'

And then I realised why Johanna's disappearance was being taken so seriously. A few months earlier there had been a vicious sex murder in Staffordshire not far from Weston. The crime created a stir because the town had been attracting publicity as a haven of civic safety. A curfew system had brought its crime figures right down and many other towns were following its example.

As a result of the murder the Home Secretary's roving Commission on Urban Violence, a tough national investigative body set up some years earlier (and dubbed 'CURV' by the tabloids purely because one of its fringe assistants was an attractive female sociologist) had been sent to aid the local police.

6

I kept a small cuttings file of sex crimes for my book and now I rummaged through it. There were a couple of detailed pieces there. Jane Triar was the name of the girl who had been raped and mutilated in a bus shelter. The police must have been very worried by the murder's potential impact because, so far as I could remember, it was the smallest crime ever handled by CURV. The Brent picket line stabbings, their last case, involved four corpses not one. Their intention in Weston was to assess the crime's effect on the community as well as to solve it. But, with so little known about the victim, who had run away from her Blackpool home some years earlier, they faced an impossible task. The newspapers made it sound as if the corpse had turned up out of thin air. There had been no arrest.

I pushed the file shut and stood there, shivering. It was colder in the flat than it should have been. I opened the door to the tiny hallway connecting the sitting room with the stairs. The front door stood slightly ajar. Yesterday's milk still lay on the step outside. The apartment block was silent and deserted.

The front door-latch is faulty and I had come in drunk the night before but, after the events of the last hour, it made me unsettled. Back in the sitting room I looked carefully around. The sofa by the window was strewn with odd books and papers. There was some kitchen debris on the table beside it and a pile of record covers stacked untidily by the speakers. It was all normally untidy.

It wasn't until I carefully inspected the papers on my desk that I knew someone had been through them.

The chapter on rape was on my typewriter where I had left it, but a whole earlier section on the nuclear family had been removed from my drawer. I could be sure of this because it was one of the few sections I had put away as complete and had no wish to change.

Now, looking round with more attention, I began to suspect that everything had been slightly rearranged: the books out of order; the centre cushion on the ageing sofa pulled out of place.

I went to my window and looked down at the frost-bound London streets. They were deserted, apart from a well-wrapped family getting out of a car a little way down. I felt strangely uneasy, guilty and curious – in that order.

The more I thought about it all, the more miserable and trapped I felt in the empty flat. For an hour I sat on the carpet with my back to the wall and thought about her. When I got up I felt better. I folded and put away my papers. I took with me a map of central England and quite a large sum of cash. I owed my memories.

The radio was playing nothing but hymns as I crossed the first northern overpass out of London.

Chapter Two

I first met Johanna when she was living in the tiny attic bedroom of a student flat in a northern university town. The bedroom contained a reproduction of Durer's *Praying Hands*, a sketch of a pretty African man she claimed to have drawn, a record player surrounded by Tamla-Motown and Swingle Singers albums, a wardrobe of expensive clothes, a table of Mary Quant make-up and a teddy bear on a narrow divan. Yet it was a fascinating room. Because the naive personality it seemed to reflect was nothing but a phantasm – not even a memory of the past, but something which had never existed.

Perhaps this was why Johanna exerted such a strong initial fascination. She was no traditional beautiful hysteric. She did not indulge in rapturous introspection or enigmatic asides. You may still – with difficulty – come across that type amongst attractive female university students, but Johanna did not correspond to it at all. Nor was she, more fashionably, fey or moody or aggressive. On the surface everything about her suggested a gentle exuberant naivety rooted in strong intelligence.

She was the kind of person that invited protection on account of a bruised but infectious gaiety. As a lover and companion, she was trusting, affectionate and eccentric with a marked emotional streak. But she had this odd thing about lying.

At first it seemed almost like a misguided sense of the dramatic. She would talk at length about incidents that had never happened, people she had never known, places she had never been. But she would lie too about which of her records were borrowed, about whether it had rained at the weekend and her first name.

Johanna's ability to fantasise any persona for herself by a simple exercise of imagination was startling. It wasn't impetuous or simple-minded and it gave her a dimension you would never have guessed from the bland English-rose innocence of her bedroom. Love-making became either total fantasy or intensely therapeutic truth-telling.

But sometimes it got more complicated. After she told me, in the strictest confidence, that her dragonish mother was in fact only a step-mother, I was sufficiently sceptical to look at her birth certificate: this story too was invented.

Johanna's relationship with her mother was an unpleasant mixture of pity, babyish adoration and terror. Physically Mrs Parver was a striking combination of austere headmistress and pantomine witch. A former actress, she was tall and wiry with a tensile strength of will that gave an almost supernatural air to her 65 years. Her proprietorial attitude towards her daughter stemmed from the prolonged absence of any male onlooker and the periodic toughness of her own life.

Johanna's father had died only months after she was born, leaving her mother some money, the option of American citizenship and a detached house, bought cheaply as a love nest while his first wife was still a problem. It had been cheap because it was on the outskirts of Weston, a small and attractive village destined, on account of a newly constructed smelting works, to become one of the more grotesque victims of sixties urban redevelopment.

I knew that at first hand because I had accompanied Jo on a rare visit home in the late sixties, while she'd still hoped her mother might come to terms with me. Even after the rows, I can remember having room for a flash of horror at the windswept nucleus of Weston's new development which was eating the old village alive.

Mrs Parver's hostility towards male approaches to her daughter might have diminished with the right man and the right overtures. But in the late sixties there was no possibility of compromise. Not between a naive student with a selfless belief in the freedom of attractive daughters and a puritanical ex-actress, privately convinced of the virtues of 'older' men.

So nobody won. The tournament ended a few years later with Jo's attempted suicide and a lot of pain.

Now driving my Mini down the deserted pock-marked motorway towards a town I hadn't seen in well over a decade, it felt almost as though I was manning the controls of a time machine.

The sky began to get dark, and my mind kept returning of

its own accord to that pile of clothes beside the road, trying to detail the items and the way they were lying. Each time I forced the screen to go blank. I didn't want to think any more about Jo, because it would only take me back into a maze of sadness and guilt.

I needed something to keep up the energy that had spurred this pilgrimage. I stopped and opened a half-empty bottle of Tequila, that Karen and I had shared on her last night. Neat, it tasted sharp and acid but left a distinct sensation.

I turned up the radio, forcing myself to try and sing along with the carol, ransacking half-lost memories for the words: 'See amid the winter snow.'

The windscreen wipers clicked obsessively in time to the beat. A rain-storm gathered intensity and darkness seemed to move in around the car. My mind began to flicker lightly over the events of the years, like a fire suddenly stoked and replenished. Various people came to sit beside me, including finally even Johanna, who sang the hymn as she stared out at the wind and the rain. I made sure she didn't talk about what had happened since I last saw her. Or why her clothes were left by the road.

After turning off a lonely stretch of ancient motorway near the Staffordshire/Shropshire border, I found my way onto a long and winding B-road which skirted across country. It was dark by then and, during the last stages of the journey, I must have been almost in a trance, because I seemed to see beams of light moving behind the trees and downwards from the sky in a kind of arc.

Then, like shapes from another world, I dimly registered the gleaming black rainwear of the police.

Chapter Three

The sergeant who peered in at me through the driving rain
was unexpectedly friendly, considering the way he was spend-
ing Christmas. His two colleagues were younger and tougher
but the sergeant did the talking.

'Sorry sir, the road's liable to flood, and we're keeping a
check on it. Are you going into Weston?'.

The flooding story was laughable, but the police still sometimes tried not to alarm the public unnecessarily. I noticed
a makeshift shack by the hedge.

'Yes I am.'

He looked at me more closely.

'Unfortunately we'll have to ask you a few questions on
account of this murder hunt. But it's a pity to freeze to death.
Can you come into the hut?'

The hut turned out to be more like a barracks than a
temporary shelter: a couple of bunks with sleeping bags, a
cooker, and a small stove which heated it adequately. I also
noted a cupboard with a stout padlock.

They ran through the usual enquiries, about me and my
movements. I showed them my press card and told them I
had been sent to cover the disappearance story. They filled
in their forms, then let me go.

Eventually I approached Weston not through the newer
urban centre but by way of the old engulfed village.

The parish church, in what had once been the main street
of the village, now looked completely lost and out of place
under the glare of the new sodium streetlights. Immediately
behind it stood a large warehouse and above it a grey spiral
of pylons and wires. Across the road an old three-storey
house, with boarded-up windows and an askew 'H' TV aerial,
still retained a sign bearing the fallacious legend 'High Street',
but it was swamped by a network of power transmission lines.

What had once been the focal pub, an old Victorian build-

12

ing, was visible halfway along. The rain had stopped by the time I got out of the car to take a look.

Peering through the main window I could just make out by the streetlight the remainder of the bar, covered in dust and bits of plaster where someone had stripped the walls. Some of the bottles behind it still survived; empties with peeling labels which had somehow evaded vandals.

Further down the road there were some newer shops and banks but the few remaining houses all appeared to be empty. The one next door to the pub had an ancient red tarpaulin over a decayed roof. The street was a miniature model of inner city desolation.

Finally, in a more residential section of the town, I found a grey three-storey hotel which seemed to be functioning normally. Ivy grew up its front like a verdant fungus, giving it that particular flavour of a retreat for the elderly, an impression contradicted only by the ancient multi-coloured sign beneath the sober main lettering, announcing 'Disco Bar'. The idea almost cheered me up in a town which seemed to commemorate Christmas about as heartily as a multiple funeral.

The room I was given was bare and uninteresting with a writing table, an old fashioned bed and a chest of drawers. The cheap black and white television in the corner worked better than the futile four channel radio system by the bed. The rules behind the door were standard, but I read them and the fire regulations just the same. I always do.

What on earth would have brought Johanna back to a town like this? Had she returned from America to stay here? Living with her clinging distraught mother, perhaps getting married here. It seemed hard to believe. She had hated the town as much as she hated being at home.

The television was playing some rural soap opera. A man and a woman were eating a meal in what looked like a farmhouse kitchen.

'I wish he wasn't so late,' said the woman. 'It's getting dark.'

'I'll put on the outside light,' said the man.

It was one of those awful serials with a built-in public service message. I turned the switch. Even the Disco Bar had to be better than this.

13

Chapter Four

From a phone-booth downstairs I called the Weston police and was put through to the same friendly sergeant.

In his polite way he was less than helpful. No, they weren't for the moment prepared to reveal where the clothes had been found because the site was still being examined. Nor could they enlighten me about the progress of the investigation, but they would be issuing a statement soon.

The call yielded only one bit of hard information. Johanna was officially described as having no next-of-kin. Her mother had died. The police were still anxious to trace where exactly she had been living.

I brooded on this last bit of news. How was it that in a comparatively small town, nobody had come forward to tell them where she lived? And if she had moved away from Weston, what was she doing here? And why didn't anyone in the rest of England come forward with an address?

I looked into the restaurant by the phone-booth where a few families, dressed in their very best clothes, ate solemnly and without much animation. By the door, a young child leaned close to his mother, quivering slightly as she fed him spoonfuls of turkey. He looked spastic or retarded. I couldn't face Christmas dinner.

The only other people in the Disco Bar, which was a tiny tinselly room with a juke box, were a teenage couple in the corner. A coke lay untouched in front of them. Their rucksacks suggested they were hitching through. After a while they broke off their whispered conversation and the girl looked round at me. She was small and rather well-featured with large brown eyes, long dark hair. The expression was half-heartedly appealing as though she were scared of her own ability to solicit pity.

'D'you know anywhere cheap we can spend the night?' she said.

14

I explained I was a stranger myself.

She kept on looking at me.

I offered them a drink and bought whiskeys at the bar from a quiet spotty youth.

While they were being poured I put a coin in the juke box and played the only decent song I could find: *Baby Let's Play House* by Elvis Presley. It stood out from the other records so oddly that I wondered what it was doing there.

The couple pounced on the drinks like stranded fish. The boy was black haired and unshaven with an attractive shy smile. His features were quite delicate under the stubble. He introduced himself as Steve, the girl was Marie. 'After Marie Lloyd my grandad says, whoever she was,' she grinned.

'What's the hitching like here?' I asked them.

'Terrible. You can't imagine,' said the boy. His accent was Tyneside but there was an odd jerkyness about the way he talked. 'Marie and I are trying to get down to Bristol. But no-one's picking up at all.'

Marie joined in, 'I reckoned we could make a detour and spend the night. But we can't find anywhere. A Bed and Breakfast told us to screw off.'

They looked at each other, and something passed between them that seemed to be pre-arranged. He got up rather artificially to go to the toilet. She looked down and swallowed, then pushed her hair back with one hand. She looked at me, her eyes still wide and sad.

'Look we're a bit desperate', she spoke slowly but decisively with a faint Liverpool accent. 'All our bread's gone on bus-fares and stuff. And we've got to get down to Bristol. Could you lend us some money? Five would see us.'

There was no mistaking her genuineness and I got out my wallet. On impulse, before handing her the five pound note, I inserted two eyes, a nose and a smiling mouth in the natural circle of the banknote above Wellington's rather pompous head. She looked at the face and laughed as she took it from me.

It was about then I noticed a small middle-aged man, standing in the doorway watching us. He went over to the bar and had a brief word with the boy before going through to the dining room. When I went up to the bar for another drink, the spotty youth looked very embarrassed,

'I'm afraid I can't sell you a drink for the lady, sir. My

15

dad's instructions.' He brought his hand up to his mouth to pick his lip. It was dry. He smelt of hair-oil.

I tried not to get angry, 'What's the matter?'.

He shuffled wretchedly: 'We have a right to refuse without a reason, sir. Not for the lady. I'm very sorry.'

There was no point in arguing. I ordered two whiskeys, gave them to the couple and told them I'd been drinking all day and had had enough. I looked back surreptitiously at the bar. The boy carefully averted his eyes. It didn't look as though he was going to interfere any more.

It turned out that when she was thirteen Marie had once visited a teenage cousin in Weston, whose family had since emigrated to Australia. The two of them looked old enough to hang around the local pubs. But that was before experimental curfews had become a fad in some of the more conservative localities. Weston had been one of the first small towns to institute one and soon trumpted its success. The town's crime figures were supposed to be among the lowest in the country. The curfews were no longer compulsory but the night-life had not recovered.

'Christmas night and it's like a fuckin' morgue. We've been round everywhere,' said Steve emphatically.

Marie seemed to agree, 'The whole place is dead. My cousin hated it here.'

'Did she know him?' I asked, pointing at the proprietor's gangly son.

'No he's only about sixteen. I think she knew his sister a little. She was our age. But most of the kids here were real prudes. No fun.'

Marie had run away from home in Merseyside the previous summer, and met up with Steve, an art student from Newcastle, a few weeks before Christmas. They'd spent virtually all their money on an abortive trip to Scotland, and were now trying to get down to Bristol where there was a flat they could use and some possibility of work.

We talked about art school and hitching and their parents. I couldn't help liking them. They reminded me of a quality I had forgotten from my own hitching days: that kind of peculiar twentieth-century honesty that only seems to come from a persistent reliance on the altruism of other people. As the evening wore on, Marie made me think of Karen far away in Finland, and I wished she was here instead of teaching

16

English beside a wood-stove. A part of me wanted to offer Marie and Steve a lift to London and forget about Johanna. But I couldn't.

Steve announced they'd have to get going. If they didn't get a lift out of town, they'd take a taxi as far as the toll-bridge on the main road where they were sure of finding a lorry. It was an unpleasant prospect on a freezing winter night.

They left, and rather furtively I went up to the bar for a last drink. I drank it quickly and sauntered out into the darkness for a short walk before bed.

Some of my anxiety had actually subsided. It was probably the whiskey. I had no sense at all of how much death there was around that night.

Chapter Five

The hotel was by far the largest building on a quiet residential street. The others were carefully sealed off from each other by minute walls and hedges. Some of the gardens had young trees planted in single rows.

It was a cold and clear night with frost settling in on the windows and the cars. I watched my breath coagulating, and decided to walk up to the end of the road and then back round the block by a parallel street I'd seen from the car. I turned the corner into the next road which was slightly narrower; the houses were new and badly-designed, all identical apart from the gardens and varieties of fencing.

My footfall echoed on the pavement. Dim lights peeped out from behind heavy blinds and shutters. The petit bourgeois atmosphere was stifling, but in view of what had happened to some other towns you could understand it.

Turning into the street that connected the two sides of the rectangle, I heard a noise. It came from one of the little detached houses a few yards to my right. A half-panting, half-whining sound. As though something was in pain or struggling. Almost like an animal. But as I stopped and listened, I realised my first impression was wrong. There was no sense of alarm. This was submissive, infantile. Its urgency was contrived, like a performance.

The light inside was dim. It wasn't until I had stared for some time that I realised the mobile blob of pink, directly in my line of vision, was a little boy's face. It was giggling and moving convulsively, resting on what I took to be a pillow beside a solitary table-light. There was something slightly wet and fleshy about his mouth, as if it had been smeared in olive oil.

He wriggled and spasmed, jerking his head against the bed, as he brought a hand up to his mouth, giving out unnerving

18

little whimpers of pleasure and pain. Somewhere in the further reaches of the house a baby was crying.

I heard the door open and the room was suddenly illuminated by an overhead light. The crimson three-piece suite and draped side-table revealed not, as I had thought, a bedroom but a suburban living room. A woman in her sixties, with heavy features stood looking at the boy who lay there quietly on the sofa, with his eyes open and his hand up to his mouth. I suppose I was expecting to witness some ritual punishment for this interrupted masturbation, but the woman's face had no expression.

It was only when his head appeared from the end of the sofa that I realised the boy had not been alone. The man moved out of view and he must have turned on a television because laughter and music suddenly erupted from somewhere close to the window.

I moved quietly back into the road, stiff and shivering from the cold. My professional curiosity was crushed by nausea. Statistics about incest do not necessarily prepare you for the real thing. I didn't know if that was what I had seen but I regretted letting my voyeuristic instinct get the better of me.

I walked briskly back to the hotel. No-one was at the desk as I went straight up the darkened stairs to my room.

I washed in the basin and looked at myself in the mirror, reflecting that it was a strange way to spend Christmas night. Watching a little boy being apparently abused by his father in the middle of nowhere for no sane reason. Happy holiday.

I dreamt that I was in my flat in London, making love to Karen. I was struggling to enter her, feeling awkward and cumbersome, but desperately wanting her response.

I looked down at her for reassurance, turning the head with my hand, and there staring up at me were the familiar pert features of the tiny girlish face in the window: the mouth slightly twisted and the tongue running over the top lip. The eyes were large and mocking but aroused.

A mob of policemen hammered on the door, shouting for the child. I woke in a throbbing sweat on the hotel bed. But the knocking got louder. I scrambled up. It was coming from the door.

I opened it and Steve stood there. For a moment I couldn't even think who he was.

'The police have busted Marie,' he said. 'They've got her.'
I felt stupid, dimly trying to register what he was saying.

'Oh hell. . . . Was she carrying anything?' I said it slowly,
supposing she was.

He shook his head vigorously: 'For soliciting, not drugs.
That's what they said. We were on the road out of here when
they picked us up. I was allowed to go.'

He had hung around the police station for hours without
any effect. There was still some Tequila left, and he looked
so worked over that I gave him the rest of it.

'You can sleep on the floor here' I found myself saying.
'We'll try and find out what's happened in the morning.'

After he'd crawled into his sleeping-bag, I lay back in bed,
wondering what else was going to happen that night.

The soliciting charge seemed inherently implausible. I
could only assume Marie or Steve had been carrying drugs
or perhaps the police were anxious about Marie's safety on
the road. They were probably getting a bit hysterical with
one search on their hands already.

Praying there would be no recurrence of my nightmare, I
shut my eyes. Sleep took a long time coming. In the corner
Steve breathed heavily. Once or twice he talked in his sleep,
and moaned in an accent even thicker than the one I'd heard.
Christmas night, I thought.

Chapter Six

The Weston and County Constabulary was more like a Dinky Toy than a building. It was long and squat and red, facing the dreary shopping centre, and fronted by corrugated half-windows through which stacked boxes were visible. The policeman behind the desk was also toytown. He was grey-haired and middle-aged with a smile that, once applied, stuck to his face like a wax impression. I had been wrong about the drugs. It seemed the Weston police were paranoid about prostitution though in this town the idea seemed comical.

'It's unfortunate, sir,' he was saying to Steve in a tone just this side of contempt. 'We try to keep it to an absolute minimum at Christmas but we have to act on complaints from the general public.'

'What complaints?' I interrupted.

He glanced at me, 'The manager complained she was soliciting in his hotel bar.' I remembered the little man's frozen glare. 'We only took her in as a warning and maybe even a bit of charity since the lady didn't have anywhere to go. She got off to a good start this morning. One of our cars was going to Birmingham and it gave her a lift down the motorway.'

'She's gone?' said Steve bewildered.

'Yes, nice and early but she left a note.' He dived below his desk. 'For one of you gentlemen I imagine. Stephen Barnes.' Steve took the note and turned from the desk.

'I gathered there was to be some sort of statement about the Parver disappearance,' I said politely.

'Can I ask who you are?' he looked at me more closely.

I produced my press card, and he examined it. Then he grinned at me, looking at his watch, licking his finger and detaching a sheet of typescript from below the desk.

'You'll have to do better than that, sir. Early birds you know. The Super held his conference at 9. You can have a

21

copy of the statement. But we've still got the site under wraps I'm afraid.

I took up the white sheet of paper, scanning it quickly.

'Where is everyone?' I asked, indicating the virtually empty building.

'The Commission are handling the investigation from the old tax office on Market Street,' he switched on his freeze-smile. 'The murder building, that is. But there's tight security over there, sir. You have to come through me for information.'

'I want to talk to someone there. Whitaker.'

His right hand began rolling a pencil up and down the desk.

'As I said, for the moment I'm responsible for the press. But I might be able to arrange an interview with one of the officers.'

'When?'

'Tomorrow at the earliest.'

'Well can't you let me see where the clothes were found today?'

'I'm sorry sir,' the pencil still rolled. 'We're not giving that information out. It wouldn't help us, it might help you.'

'I understand from whoever I spoke to on the phone last night that something had happened.' That sort of lie can sometimes produce results.

'Read the statement, sir, it's all there.'

As I had already seen the phrase 'no new developments' I wasn't about to take his advice. A few years earlier this kind of police reticence would have been unlikely, but since the race defence leagues and the coalition, many of the police force's tactics were noticeably changed. They were more se-cretive about minor matters and more inclined to small news blackouts or else the release of relevant information to a few favoured journalists who could be useful. I wasn't all that surprised, but I was frustrated and it made me forget about Marie's harassment until Steve handed me her note on the steps outside.

It was written on a sheet of scrap paper. 'Stevie,' it said in a sloping black biro, 'I've got out thank God and I'm getting a lift south now. Got the fiver, so I hope you're OK for bread. I don't know if you're ahead of me. Take care Jordie. Love Marie.'

I asked why she didn't come to the hotel, it was a silly question.

'She wouldn't know where I was.' Steve said.

Despite my protestations, he wasn't interested in making any kind of complaint to the police, so I insisted on taking him for a late breakfast at the hotel.

Over soggy ham rolls and coffee, Steve revealed rather dejectedly that he and Marie had been in a middle of a row the night before when the police arrived. In the circumstances, the sudden interruption had been doubly traumatic, and now Steve suspected she had walked out on him. But a re-reading of the note gave him some encouragement and he was pleased when I offered to take him to the motorway.

The weather was gloomy and overcast, but too cold for rain. The drive took longer than I really wanted.

When we reached the access road I lent him a couple of quid, and took a contact number in Bristol. It wasn't just that I liked them, though I did. I thought it might make a good story: 'Provincial Vice Snoopers: A Couple's Ordeal.' It isn't often you can place something in the pulp Sundays which might actually do some good.

As I was letting him off, I had a sudden intuition that I should drive south with him, leaving my memories to fester. But I rejected it. Crossing the over-viaduct back to the town, I could see him, a tiny speck by the side of one of the entry roads.

Approaching Weston by the main road, I had to admit that its main new development seemed a little more complete than it had been on my last visit. There was less mind-numbing hardware, and the air was not so burdened with the smell of diesel; the grass was greener.

But it was still the end of the world.

The whole mish-mash of housing blocks and factories and shops looked as though it had been thrown angrily onto a nursery floor by some giant saturnine child. The place was joined and arranged according to every conceivable co-ordinating principle except logical necessity. The high-rise flats perched on a windy and desolate upsurge of hill, cut off, even from the shopping centre, by a vast and depopulated car-park. Below it the industrial estate had literally engulfed the old village. There were no pathways, simply paved gaps between structures, with long tarmac valleys for roads. Even the spaces of cropped grass were spun so finely around the concrete that they became its material extension, a green inorganic fungus.

I parked my car beside one of the newest buildings. It was a town hall. In its original reconstruction Weston had evidently been squeezed on corporate amenities; when the money came, the will had gone. The energy crisis only emphasised the town's geographical isolation.

The shopping concourse was a plain concrete precinct. I walked along it, past the Medical Eye Centre, the Treasure Music Shop and Hepworths. It was Boxing Day but some of the shops were open and a few women were buying bread and newspapers. The whole centre was designed with a complete ignorance of its aeronautic liabilities. The wind howled around the shoppers like a small hurricane, forcing everyone to adopt a posture that neatly inhibited any kind of social intercourse.

I bought a copy of the local paper and entered a small coffee bar marked 'Ron Di Voo'. A fat old woman was the only other customer.

The local paper's headline was 'Referee Attacked' but it had been printed before the disappearance. I turned my attention to the police statement, full of predictable stuff about 'urgent enquiries' and the anxious tracing of hypothetical motorists.

I finished my coffee and drove down to Market Street. It was an ordinary shopping street, the only alternative to the concrete precinct, and not far from the old village High Street. The tax building, now the murder HQ, was a large three-storey building next door to the Co-op, and it looked busy. A policeman was stationed at the door.

The only meagre clue I had was the house where Johanna and her mother used to live, and I turned in that direction. The house was in the nearest thing that the town still had to a middle-class ghetto. A leafy enclave of lamp posts and trees, on the non-industrial side of the old village, which shrouded a broad maze of intersecting residential streets.

There were signs of decay but it was still much the smartest section. On one wall I even saw a tall and vicious run of barbed wire, looming high over a small garden. The murder had taken its toll in paranoia.

I had been driving around for about ten minutes before I

24

saw it. An over-ornate late Victorian structure, which settled uneasily into its tiny grounds, with a frontage like a lop-sided face.

I stopped a short distance away and walked back down the tree-lined road. There were no cars in front of the house and it seemed deserted. I looked at the brown front door and remembered that on my last visit it was unused and separated off by a screen. Above it a large round porthole-type window added to the general facial effect.

As I walked up the path towards the side door, I looked up at the window half-expecting to see Mrs. Parver's hawk-like features glaring down.

The side door of the house was ajar. There was no bell. I paused there, gazing at the back lawn which led down to an overgrown pond.

I was about to knock when I caught the sound of voices from somewhere inside. They sounded like a man and a girl. I strained to hear.

'It's as if she *were* dead,' the woman said, suddenly louder. 'I wish she was. I wish she was in the ground and we could go and put flowers on her.' Then she broke into sobs, and a male voice tried to comfort her.

I looked around nervously, half-expecting to see an enraged neighbour, appalled by this invasion of privacy. 'It would have been better than breaking up her family,' the voice said. 'Much much better.'

Curiosity finally overcame fear and I banged loudly on the door. The voices continued, unfaltering and oblivious.

Otherwise nothing happened at all.

Feeling like a thief, I took a step forward into the small kitchen. It was cluttered with the cream-coloured decor of the fifties. There was even a mangle with yellowing wooden rollers. The voices continued. I looked out into the hall, which was covered with the debris of children. Broken toys, assorted clothes and pairs of shoes.

The voices were coming from an open door leading off the hall to the right which I remembered as the sitting room. Opposite the sitting room, an elaborate screen, perversely shuttered off the front door. That was the same, but I couldn't be sure if anything else was. I moved along the wall until I could see into the sitting room.

The voices were coming from a colour television, which

25

played pointlessly to no audience that I could see. I recognised a further episode of the soap opera from the previous evening: a handsome son was comforting his mother as the father looked on. The room was as untidy as the hall, and like the kitchen it seemed over-full, the furniture strewn with clothes, a cap pistol on the carpet, a heap of toy bricks by the television. I wondered how many kids it took to overrun a house this size.

Back in the hall I noted the phone number. Then in the certainty that I was alone, I went to have a look upstairs.

Three doors led off the first landing. The first opened onto a flight of rickety wooden steps which connected with the split-level loft. Behind the second lay a big bedroom which looked parental, with a large wardrobe and bed and two old-style dressing-tables. A little girl's nightdress hung incongruously over one of the chairs.

The nearer dressing-table had some papers and loose ends on it, and a cheaply framed picture of a middle-aged couple surrounded by children. Their faces were completely unfamiliar. I looked through the papers: there was an income-tax form addressed to R. G. Sutton.

Quite clearly the house had changed hands. I felt superfluous and silly, but I kept looking out of pure curiosity. There were a few scrappy letters and bills, a post office savings book, a union card related to the smelting works. All very mundane. I felt mean and out of place going through the stuff.

Under the union card, a plain brown envelope lay open. Inside was a snapshot face down; I don't know why I took it out.

In the frozen moment of recognising Johanna – paler and older, but unmistakable – I heard someone enter the hall downstairs.

Chapter Seven

It's not easy to pass yourself off as a caller when you're in someone's bedroom, rifling their personal papers.

I slipped the snapshot into my pocket and moved onto the landing, as silently as the creaking floorboards would allow. The hall looked empty until I realised that three small children were huddled by the sitting room door. One broke away from whatever they were examining and went in, and an older kid came out of the kitchen and moved past them into the sitting room. Another wandered over to the wall, carrying what looked like a pencil.

It looked as though he was going to write on the surface but instead he began aimlessly pushing the pencil into a cavity in the wall. The children had a self-obsessed air, preoccupied but not contented.

A middle-aged woman who I recognised from the framed photo in the bedroom crossed the hall. A girl followed, blonde and big with the lumpen air of someone who's just hit puberty a little squarely. She looked pregnant, but it might have been just fat.

They disappeared into the sitting room. I was contemplating the possibility of a run past the children in the hall, when the sitting-room door opened and the father came out.

He frightened the life out of me.

There was the same monolithic quality which was apparent in his children, but it contained something else, a kind of coarseness.

He certainly looked more grotesque than in the picture. A wide paunch, a round fat face under thin black hair and a heavy broad-shouldered gait. From above, I could see the top of his head glistening with sweat.

He glanced at the children for a moment and then, to my horror he turned to climb the stairs. As noiselessly as possible, I retreated into the attic staircase.

27

There was a tiny click as I pulled the door to. The man paused within a few inches of me, and I could hear him breathing heavily.

Then he moved towards the bedroom.

There was silence. I risked opening the door and slipped out onto the landing. The hall seemed empty so I tiptoed to the top of the stairs.

The children had gone. There was no sign of anyone. I crept down the stairs, which creaked a little. The sitting-room door was open and my path across the hall would be visible from there. But so far as I could tell there was no-one in the kitchen. I took one step forward off the stairs, then another.

I was just on the point of breaking towards the kitchen when the blonde girl came out of the sitting room and looked at me.

She jumped, but instead of crying out or challenging me, she faltered and her hand went down between her legs in a pathetic gesture of self-defence.

I was so taken aback that, for a moment, I didn't do anything at all but stare. Close-up I could see little scratches on her hand.

Then she cried out and I ran across the hall into the empty kitchen. The outside door was closed. For an awful moment I thought it was locked, but I fumbled it open.

I was sure I heard someone coming down the stairs, but without looking round, I took the path as fast as I could. By the corner of the gate, where the drive met the road, I slipped on a patch of unmelted frost and fell heavily, jarring my hands and knees. I scrambled to the car, limping and cursing.

As I pulled away I glanced in the rear mirror and saw the man running out of the gate. He had something in his hand.

I remembered his daughter's cowed gesture. The sort of father who should have gone out with the Victorian era; yet battered families keep reappearing for medical examination as proof that they haven't. I breathed with relief as I took the first bend in the road.

But the joke was on me.

Fifty yards ahead, the road turned into a dead-end.

Another glance in my mirror told me the man hadn't followed. In that case either he was waiting or he might even have called the police.

I turned around and edged forward in second, my foot

ready to hit the accelerator. I didn't want to take the bend by the house at speed in case he'd got really nasty and blocked the road. There would be even more explaining to do if I wrecked his car as well.

But the road outside the house was quiet. Nothing moved. I picked up speed and changed into third, staying on the far side of the road from the house. I wondered whether the police would bother to investigate if he called them.

It was fortunate for me that I saw his outline a split second before he intended. He was crouched by a tree opposite his drive, knowing my attention would be directed to the other side of the road. As he sprang I swerved, but he managed to get my door open and lunged down at me.

A sharp pain scored my right arm and I glimpsed what looked like a screwdriver in his hand. The wheel spun, I stamped the brakes, then accelerated hard. The man had failed to get a proper foothold and he was out of the car with the door swinging crazily to as I drove blindly away. With one hand on the wheel and the other nursing my shoulder I headed back into the town.

When I was sure I was not being followed, I parked in an inconspicuous street and examined my injury. Most of the blow's impact had been dispelled by the speed of the car. But it had ripped through my jacket and jersey and left a painful bruise. The man certainly valued his privacy.

Later, installed in a tiny cupboard-like pub at the end of the street, I took out Johanna's picture.

It was a four by four snapshot, slightly blurred and lacking any real detail. But the face, especially the eyes, were unmistakable. She was getting out of a car and staring straight at the camera. It didn't look as if she was aware of being photographed but I couldn't be sure. Then I saw the words printed neatly on the back corner: 'Sutton family, if seen call Weston Police at 46806.'

My disappointment was intense.

I had been all set to implicate Sutton in some diabolical kidnapping. But all this proved was that the police had been quick to release Johanna's picture.

And Sutton was probably just a sadistic nut, the kind that takes potshots at burglars.

But did this mean the police expected Johanna to return to her old house? The more I thought about that, the odder it

29

seemed. To expect her to leave her clothes by the roadside and wander back to a house she hadn't lived in for years, naked?

I sipped my whiskey. Police move in conventional ways. Maybe they were just covering every base and the old house was one of them. But it was the thoroughness of their search that took me aback. Within hours of finding her clothes they had got through to me, an obscure ex-lover. Were they telling the whole truth about her disappearance?

After a few warm-up remarks I tried Johanna's picture on the elderly publican who had served me drinks. But I might as well not have bothered. He was both unforthcoming and disdainful.

Chapter Eight

By the time I got back to the hotel, thirty-six hours of virtual sleeplessness were beginning to catch up with me. The girl behind the desk went away looking worried when I told her I wanted to see her father. Then, after a moment, the little bald man came down the stairs. He smiled but his face was flushed. The smiling aggressive type, I felt sorry for his children.

'Can I help you sir?' he said unctuously. His accent was pure Home Counties Suburban. Later I discovered that he'd moved from Pinner in the 1950s. I put my journalist's card down on the desk as one of the old people, who seemed to live in the hotel, was shuffling past.

'Yes, you can tell me why you had an innocent girl arrested in the middle of the night. Or were you just excited by her smell?'

It was meant to embarrass him and it seemed to work. His face turned a darker shade of puce and he ushered me nervously towards the bar-lounge.

'I don't think you understand, sir,' he said. His voice was oddly soft and throaty, but the eyes still flashed dangerously as we sat down. 'You see we had a bit of trouble here over the summer. Some girls started using this place.' He hesitated. 'Using it, well, as a pick-up point. It became very difficult for a time.'

I waited.

'Well, they were coming into the bar alone, you know, without any men. It was bound to cause a disturbance.'

I resisted the temptation to be rude: 'But who were these girls?' I said, feigning sympathy.

'I'd never seen them before. But you see when I saw the girl last night I thought . . . well, she might be starting something like that again!

'Had you ever seen her before?'

31

'No, never.'

'And yet you were prepared to have her arrested.'

He looked at me sullenly. 'I simply reported her presence to the police.'

'Who simply came and arrested her.'

His lips puckered: 'I understand the young lady was allowed to leave this morning.'

I could have got angrier but I was interested in something that lay behind his priggish cruelty, a quality of parochialism I couldn't quite fathom. 'I'm following up anything I can find,' I said. 'Do you think that any of the girls who came in here were connected with the murder or the disappearance?'

Then he laughed. It was a nasty laugh, prissy yet rasping, with a mock innocence about it. 'Yes Jane Triar was one of them but I only found that out afterwards. I didn't know the girls who hung around and you won't find anyone who did. Frankly most of us were more upset that it happened here than who it happened to.'

He wiped an imaginary speck of dust off the table with his hand, looking me straight in the eye for once.

'And Johanna Parver?' I said.

'I'm not familiar with the name,' he said looking away. I thrust the picture under his nose but he shook his head.

'Well can you put me on to someone who knew Jane Triar?' I asked.

'I told you,' he said with irritation, 'No-one knew her, She would be here on her own or with another girl I'd never seen. And even the men who left with them wouldn't admit it. The police have been through it all already. She's gone, good riddance.' He got to his feet: 'Now if you'll excuse me it's nearly time to open up the bar and I've a lot to do.'

I asked him if I could examine the hotel register. With a muttered complaint, he agreed. What he had told me seemed such a pack of prejudices, I hoped the register would provide something more concrete.

There wasn't a lot there. Mainly men's names, travelling salesmen I assumed. People passing through. But then I noticed an entry for the previous August.

The writing was neat and printed, anonymous. But the name struck a chord in my head. 'Bree Daniels,' it said.

I asked my red-faced friend, who was fussing elaborately

with some bar-stocks. And for the first time he was actually rude.

'Stupid question,' he snapped. 'I can't remember everyone who passes through. I haven't the faintest idea who she was.' And he turned to swear at his daughter to come and help him.

Now my curiosity was really aroused. A name as unusual as 'Bree' isn't exactly male or female. Yet he'd said 'she'. And there was something about the way he'd reacted, which suggested fear.

I was still inclined to dismiss most of what he told me as rampant sexual paranoia. That would explain his ludicrous attitude towards Marie and Jane Triar. But who was Bree Daniels?

Nursing my shoulder, I returned to my room with some food I'd bought and lay down on the bed, thinking about the day, and how the further I got into this town, the grimmer it seemed. For about the twentieth time I wished I could talk to Karen about it, and tried to imagine her Finnish Christmas. It's pitiful that you always miss someone most when things are bad.

My thoughts returned to the previous summer – before Karen decided to go away – long bouts of work interrupted by manic socialising as, by chance, a succession of friends descended on our small flat. Having close friends to stay in a confined space is like getting drunk. Hilarious for a few nights, but it wears. At the end we were both exhausted and, although the teaching job in Finland had always been a vague option, I was blind to the fact that at some point in the summer Karen had decided to go through with it. My protestations were late enough to be merely insulting, and I had to choke them back.

I had only intended to rest for a few minutes as I lay there thinking of her. But I'd hardly slept the previous night and soon slipped into a repetitive dream. So I didn't even hear about what they had done to Johanna till the following morning.

Chapter Nine

I heard the news from a journalist friend in London called John Platt. I had rung him first thing in the morning because if anyone could give me some real background on the Jane Triar murder I know that it would be John. Most crime reporters have had to work so closely with the police in recent years that their work shades into PR for Scotland Yard. But John had managed to maintain a degree of independence. I explained to him how hard it was getting anywhere near the CURV operation.

'It always is,' he said. 'But you're sitting on top of this new one now. Any leads?'

'Not really,' I said; 'I'm not even sure the disappearance is connected with the Triar murder.'

There was a long pause.

'We can't be talking about the same thing. I mean the Parver girl's corpse?'

I felt like someone had stuck a finger in my throat.

'They found parts of her yesterday morning. It was on the news last night,' he went on, 'and in the paper today.'

With difficulty I collected my thoughts as he read me his story over the phone.

The police statement had been made at 4 pm the previous afternoon, at about the time I was playing Goldilocks in the house. The mutilated body had been found by a police search-party in the early hours of the morning in a clump of trees five miles out of the town, about three miles from where they found her clothes. The missing woman was raped and severely mutilated. She appeared to have died only a few hours before she was found. By the end of my questioning, John had got the message that something was wrong. I agreed to phone him as soon as I came back to London.

When I got to the police station, I took its steps three at a time and immediately felt the change of atmosphere. It reminded me of a movie set that has been suddenly activated. In the background, doors opened and people crossed corridors, carrying sheets of paper. A couple of policemen stood talking at the bottom of the stairs, and two men with notepads, who must have been local reporters, were leaving as I entered.

The effect was not excessive but it increased my anger. And there, in front of me, at the PR desk was the same smiling grey-haired man. He opened his mouth in greeting but I didn't let him speak.

'Why didn't you tell me about the girl yesterday, that her body had been found?'

His smile gave way to a look of concern. 'I'm sorry sir. The news wasn't released until the afternoon. We were making a last effort to trace some next-of-kin.

'But if you knew, why didn't you give me an idea?'

His face changed gear again. This time it was humility with a hint of recrimination and earnestness. But his right hand still turned the pencil round and round.

'I'm afraid I didn't know,' he continued, 'or I'd have told you to expect a statement. Sometimes communications get fouled. It's unfortunate.'

It suddenly seemed to me, watching this man's expression that I wasn't dealing with a policeman at all, but with a rather skilled professional actor. The change of tone was so expert, the careful adjustment of the face, pitch and emphasis. This, and the thought of Johanna, and the pain in my shoulder made me angry enough to want to tear out his fine grey hair; I fully expected it was a stage-wig which would come away in my hand. Instead I lost my temper completely.

'Listen I've been here thirty-six hours,' I said. 'A girl is arrested for talking to me in a bar. There's a man molesting a kid in his front-room. I nearly get my arm sawed off by someone with a screwdriver. That's fine. But now you tell me that a woman was raped and murdered under your noses yesterday morning, even though the whole town is sewn up so tight you can practically hear people wetting themselves.'

For a moment there was a flash of interest in his eyes, but only for a moment. Then he looked resigned and unhappy.

'Well I'll try and let you talk to Whitaker, sir. He's up to his neck, but I'll see what I can do.'

He went away and came back looking pleased. 'Whitaker

says that in the circumstances he's prepared to give you an unofficial briefing, and he'll take you out to the murder site tomorrow at three.' His eagerness at this development seemed so genuine that I wondered whether I had been doing him an injustice. But his tone suddenly changed. 'And I'm to ask you if you have a photograph.'

The words were unnerving. The photograph was in my breast pocket. I had not intended to make any reference at all to what had happened the day before, in the house, until my temper got the better of me.

'What?' I stalled weakly.

'I realise it must be painful for you, sir,' he said gently, 'but Whitaker was wondering if you had an old picture of the deceased. We're having difficulty digging a good one out.'

I was taken aback: 'No, it was a long time ago. . . .'

It was feeble, but it seemed to satisfy him. I had no way of knowing if my visit to the house had been reported.

'At three then,' the smiler continued tactfully. 'And sir, those other matters you mentioned,' he shouted amicably after me. 'We're quite willing to look into any complaints.'

I spent the rest of that day in fruitless investigation. In retrospect, my preoccupation with the questions surrounding Johanna's death was a blatant attempt to avoid the emotions it had aroused. A part of me had reacted as intensely as if we had still been living together.

In the evening I combed the papers in the Disco Bar. There was not much that I did not already know. The Mail pounced on the fact that the movements of both girls before their deaths were shrouded in mystery. Jane Triar was known to have attended an extra-curricular course at a London drama school two years before. Johanna had been living in America with her sick mother, but she had re-entered the country after her mother died. It was also known, via a major insurance company, that Johanna had collected quite a substantial sum from her mother's life insurance in cash. Was it possible, the paper drooled, that both girls were involved in drugs-pushing with some avenging Manson-type leader? But the writer finally had to admit his theory was less likely than straight sex-crime.

I agreed with him. No proof existed that the girls even knew each other. And I happened to know that Johanna preferred to hoard cash rather than use a bank account. That might make robbery a motive but there was nothing mysterious about her asking for money in notes.

None of the papers carried a photo of Johanna. But by far the most unnerving aspect was the appearance of the clothes, and the general assumption that she had been a prisoner for some hours before her death. It was hard to stomach the possibility that Johanna was still alive when I reached Weston, that my car might even have passed the spot where she was being held. The delay gave the murder a horrifying cold-bloodedness.

These reflections were cut short by the awareness that I was being studied by a man at the far corner of the bar. He had silvery spectacles, executive-style 'long' hair and a loud three piece suit; an unread Harold Robbins paperback lay beside him.

'Nowt entertainment here eh?' he said at last.

His Yorkshire accent immediately set him apart on this side of the country.

'No it's pretty grim.' He seemed pleased to learn I wasn't local.

'Still I'm eternally hopeful,' he said, sliding down from his stool, and grasping me rather spongily by the hand. 'Fred Stevens, salesman from Leeds,' he said. 'Building materials.' He handed me a card with shaking fingers. Evidently he had already drunk a good deal. I caught myself guessing how his conversation would go: a few Irish jokes, some baleful remarks about the economy and then dirty stories. The prospect filled me with misery and, after the first anecdote about a postman in a convent, I was on the point of making my excuses when he looked dolefully round the empty bar.

'I'm very disappointed tonight,' he said emphatically. 'Very disappointed. You see I had high hopes of a bit of you know. . .' He gave a gasp of mock passion and then burst out laughing. 'I'd have paid for it.'

'Here?' I said incredulously, remembering the landlord's story.

'Listen,' he leaned forward confidentially. 'A friend of mine was round this way six months ago. He swore to me there was a regular on the game did it for virtually nothing. A few drinks and a couple of quid. They went to his room.'

He lowered his tone still further and his breath fell unpleasantly on my face, 'I've heard the whole thing about a dozen times. Fantastic tits. All but did it in the road.'

He broke up into wheezy laughter and took another sip from his drink. 'Here, can you imagine?' Then he looked wistful again. 'I had an introduction and everything. But there's no sign of her now.'

'Do you know who she was?' I said.

'Oh God everything. . . . It's kept us going for weeks.'

His hand went up to his chest in a macabre rubbing motion. He had obviously been geared up for this evening for ever: weeks of fantasising and masturbation, of morning hard-ons and evening sweat. I couldn't see him as a murderer but his slobbering appetite tallied sickeningly with everything else. Up to now I'd more or less utterly rejected the notion of prostitution here, discounting it as prudish innuendo. But here was confirmation from a completely unpuritanical source.

I tried to get more concrete information out of him but, even in his more sober moments, all he could offer was ribald gossip. Eventually he relapsed into sentiment about his wife and family. At closing time we went upstairs together and he solemnly shook my hand.

But like everyone else in this town he had his curtain-line saved up, though this one couldn't have been prepared. The drunkenness, the blood-shot eyes, even the hint of an erection were biological guarantees of spontaneity.

'It's funny,' he said, swaying towards me. 'Jackie had it all set up for me. He even managed to worm her real name out of her . . . a funny boy's name.' He mused for a moment. 'Jo. Jo the goer.'

He winked and turned away, staggering slightly. He nearly fell before he made his bedroom, but just at that moment I don't think I would have noticed if he had started walking on air.

Chapter Ten

The more I thought about it back in my room, the less I was able to comprehend.

Many lurid or conventional scenarios for Johanna had run through my head in the last few years. I could imagine her as everything from a bar hostess to a librarian, a high-class hustler to a respectable married woman. But a small-town prostitute?

For one thing, as a sexual researcher I knew the phenomenon scarcely existed outside of male folk-fantasy. Certainly there were flexible amateurs who could attract lucrative custom via contact magazines. But the idea of professionals openly plying their trade on the streets of England's smaller inland towns like Weston or Corby or Hemel Hempstead seemed about as real to me as brothels disguised as cinemas. They were part of the male mythology of sex. And now evidence was accumulating, not merely that the fantasy was real, but that it might even be the reason for Johanna's murder.

I thought about Johanna sexually. She was comparatively uninhibited and she had a hysterical, almost dramatic flair. She would be expert at manipulating other people's fantasies. But there was no compulsive aspect to her sexuality; and more importantly she lacked the dogged stoicism which seems to be the standard trait among female (and male) prostitutes. In fact, everything I knew about her confirmed that only privation of the most desperate and catastrophic kind could possibly have led her into prostitution.

And how did that square with the salesman's story? 'Did it for virtually nothing.' Even if his information were highly coloured, it was unlikely that two businessmen would mislead each other over the price of the transaction.

In fact it was the very bravado of the description, the recklessness of the price, that squared most emphatically with Jo's character. But if she wasn't doing it for money, why was she doing it? It almost sounded like contempt. As if she were mocking the man without his knowing it. But it still made no sense.

And if Jo was her 'real' name, what was her alias? Was it Bree Daniels?

Then I remembered the photograph.

The spotty boy was still downstairs washing glasses. He was surprised to see me and, when I thrust the photograph at him, he looked terrified.

'Have you seen her before?' I asked.

He glanced at the door as though he suspected some sort of trick.

I changed tack and smiled. 'I'm a journalist. It's just a matter of a story we're doing.'

He looked even more taken aback.

'You dad said it was OK,' I lied in desperation. That seemed to work.

He screwed up his eyes and stared silently at the photo for a long time. 'That's one of the girls used to come in here last summer.' Self-consciously he added, 'Not since the murder.'

He didn't know where she had come from. 'Used to watch her,' he mumbled, his eyes faintly tumescent and furtive.

'The name. Did you know it?'

'Oh yes' he said looking back down. 'It was Bree Daniels.' I took a breath.

'Who knew her?'

'No-one. She came and went.' He sounded like his father.

'Did you talk to her?'

'Only once,' he said, biting his bottom lip, slightly ashamed. 'She gave me that record for the juke-box. Said it was Weston's record.'

'Which record?' But I knew.

'The Elvis one.' He picked up his cloth and prepared to resume work.

At that point his father appeared through the door. When he saw the two of us, his face began to redden again. I tried to intercept the outburst, by holding up the picture: 'So you did know Bree Daniels?'.

But his attention was focused on the boy. He walked towards him and the kid cowered visibly under his raised fist. He brought his knuckles down hard on top of his son's head.

40

The boy just took it, standing there dumbly as the fist came down twice more. He didn't even cry out.

Finally the boy walked blindly towards the door with one hand over his head and his eyes streaming. He stumbled slightly on his way out and only then a sound came out of him, a little gasp for breath.

The father watched him go before he turned to me. 'Don't interfere with my family or you'll have to leave at once.' It was spoken with almost insane normality rather as if he were saying: 'Don't put your feet up on the furniture.'

I looked at him mutely for a moment before holding up the photo. 'Bree Daniels?' I said.

He glared at it.

'Yes, that's her. Another of them. What of it?'

'Why did you lie?'

'Because we were stupid enough to give her a room one night, that's why.' He shifted an ash-tray. 'It was before we quite realised what she was. I didn't want you to advertise I let a whore stay in my hotel, did I?'

'Did she know Jane Triar?'

'Oh yes. Bet she got out pretty fast after that'

'You don't understand who this is?' I said. Watching his reactions microscopically and pointing at the picture. 'This is Johanna Parver.'

He seemed genuinely surprised and he looked at the picture properly for the first time. 'So another one of them's been done have they? Well well well.'

'Can't you tell me who her friends were?'

He raised his eyes to heaven and went over to turn off the lights.

'Listen mate, how many times? No-one knew her. Especially not Bree Daniels. You're wasting your time. Go back and find where they came from, that's what you want to do.'

'But you knew her name?' I said. It was a last desperate effort.

'No we didn't, did we? We only knew a phoney one. And she was always shouting it around. You couldn't miss it. No-one will tell you anything.'

And he held the door open for me to go back into the hall.

41

Chapter Eleven

B-B-B-B-B-B Baby baby baby
B-B-B-B-B-B Baby baby baby
Come back baby I wanna play house with you

The obsessive repetition of Presley's *Baby Let's Play House*
haunted me for the rest of that night. It was the perfect
evocation not only of Weston's mindless intersection of gloomy council blocks and closeted villas, but also its over-pro-
tected children, silent victims of the town's obsession with
defensible space. I thought of Johanna slotting it on the juke
box in mockery but, if there was some hidden code behind
the song, it escaped me.

At breakfast I was surprised by a phone call from Steve in
Bristol. Marie had not reappeared and he was now sure he'd
been given the elbow. I reassured him clumsily but somewhere I felt a small nagging anxiety.

That morning an official press conference was given by
Andrew Paines, a former Chief Constable of the Staffordshire
Police, who was now one of the chief officers of CURV and
personally responsible for the Weston investigation.

I arrived late and had some difficulty getting in because
everyone else had evidently been cleared in advance. Squatted
at the back, I was in time to hear Paines give a brief and
highly technical account of Johanna's injuries and then make
a public appeal for help.

His appearance surprised me, thin and good-looking with
a modish blue waistcoat under his plain well-fitting suit. His
hair was cut just above the collar and he looked young for a
senior policeman. I found out later that he had been one of
the sixties' few public school recruits.

When I managed to squeeze in a question about the delay
in reporting the discovery of the body, it was greeted with
contemptuous glances. Apparently Paines had begun his

42

statement by answering precisely this question and most of the eyes in the room took in my crumpled appearance with the sort of group disdain that senior journalists affect as easily as any other coterie.

It was an unpleasant feeling. But, after pausing to look at me, Paines himself was civil enough. Positive identification of the body had taken some time and they had made a last-minute effort to trace any next-of-kin before releasing the news.

I was able to get harder information at my three o'clock appointment with Detective Superintendant Whitaker, who turned out to be a middle-aged man in a battered raincoat with a defiantly military bearing. Whereas the desk-sergeant seemed almost showy and Paines was crisply middle-class, Whitaker looked scruffy and down-at-heel but intelligent.

For the time being, I discovered, Whitaker was seconded to the Commission as a crime detection officer, but before that, like Paines, he had worked in the Staffordshire police. His knowledge of the area and the local force had made him one of the key men in the present investigation.

'I gather you were a bit misinformed the other day,' he said amiably as he ushered me into his Rover. 'The body was in a hell of a mess and we couldn't release anything until we were sure. We can talk on the way out there.'

He drove me out of town on his own, without a driver, on a winding road parallel to the one I'd taken on Christmas night. I knew from the map that eventually it joined the motorway further south.

'According to what we can make out,' he began, 'it must have happened late on Christmas night. She was raped more than once. There was extensive mutilation after death. Especially to the head. The jaw was practically cut-out. But the cause of death seems to have been several stab wounds.'

'Doesn't that mean a search party may have been close when it happened?'

'Yes,' he said gloomily. 'But the pathologist is insistent about the time. The man must have kept her all day and some of the night, quite close to where we were searching. But the countryside is riddled with passable farm-roads which makes it difficult to cordon. We were concentrating round the clothes, which turned up in a lay-by on this road. In fact they really threw us off.'

He spoke loudly, in a slight Midlands accent, as if he were used to pitting his voice against heavy noise. And he reproduced exactly the rather folksy pendantry of the long-serving police officer.

For some reason this unnerved me. It was again rather like being in the presence of an impeccable actor. I found myself wanting him to reveal some unlikely detail or unexpected twist. That he hated the police force or that his son played chess for England. But he didn't. Instead he turned and asked me about my relationship with the deceased.

I explained that I'd been close to her some years ago, but hadn't seen her since. 'I wouldn't even know how to get in touch with her,' I added truthfully. 'Is there no next-of-kin?'

Whitaker shrugged: 'There may be a cousin somewhere in Florida. But we've almost given up. You may have gathered that almost everything we've got on both these girls is a year out of date.'

'So you still have no idea where Johanna was living?'

'I don't think she lived anywhere regular. That may be one of the reasons why it happened.'

He was waiting for a reaction, but I played innocent, staring out at the passing scenery before replying. 'Do you think she was sleeping rough then?' I asked carefully.

'With all due respect' he said woodenly. 'I just think she may not have been too fussy who she slept with. It's amazing how often that causes problems in cases like this. It makes our job a lot more difficult nowadays.'

He yawned ostentatiously. 'Believe me if young people were a little more choosey about who they went to bed with. . . .'

I cut in, 'Have you ever heard of Bree Daniels?'

He shrugged, 'It was just a name she used. But we still can't get a single customer to come forward. That's always the trouble when some maniac takes it into his head to go for a professional.'

I was tempted to challenge his wretched police-stereotype of Johanna as a ripped whore but something stopped me. I lacked any hard evidence to contradict him except a mixture of sexological theory and instinct, and I was not going to start explaining that. So I changed the subject, 'How did you manage to trace me so quickly on Christmas Day?'

Whitaker smiled for the first time as he took a sharp right onto a road which ran uphill, 'I wish it was all as easy as that, sir,' he said. 'You see Mrs. Parver made a number of complaints against you at one time. In connection with her daughter. She was a bit of a nutter so they never followed them up. But they are still on record and it seemed an obvious place to start.'

'But what became of the Parver house?' I asked.

Whitaker fiddled elaborately with the heater switch.

'They sold it,' he said finally. 'While they were in America.'

'Oh,' I tried to sound disinterested. 'Who to?'

'Council bought it,' he said casually. 'At one time we had a theory Miss Parver might have gone back there. You know, the homing instinct. But the family who live there now never saw her. We asked them to keep a look out.' That seemed to solve the riddle of the photo. I was still curious to know why the police were not releasing it to the press but I couldn't see a way to ask him without revealing the incident in the house.

The murder setting was appropriately desolate. We drove off the road up a cart-track and then walked about five hundred yards to a small copse of trees, which stood on a high point where the land sloped down most steeply to the north, from which the town was clearly visible. The hillside slanted away into fields on the other side and, to the south-east, the road we had driven along, where her clothes had been found, was just discernible.

Looking to the west I saw that Whitaker's point about the farm roads was a fair one. At least three tracks cut their way through the fields and hedges. Anyone here would have a clear vantage-point for miles around and the track below subdivided into a maze of just-negotiable lanes.

Two policemen in uniform guarded the copse and nodded at Whitaker. We walked to the small clump of trees where the body had lain. The thin line of white paint, marking its outline, looked stark and unnatural against the undergrowth.

'She was completely unrecognisable,' Whitaker remarked unnecessarily and then began a desultory chat with the policeman. I walked off a little way.

The darkness was beginning to settle and I stared back at the dreary orange lights of Weston as the wind began to whip up around the trees. Now for the first time I attempted to face the reality of Johanna's death and found I didn't know what to do with it.

Losing someone at a long distance of time is like losing

45

someone in a dream. I'd once heard about a prisoner of war, separated from his wife for five years, who came home to find that she had died of a lung infection the week before. I felt a bit like that now; as if Johanna's death was just another extension of her absence and the knowledge of *why* it had happened could bring her back. All the emotion lay trapped inside me.

Even when I forced myself to confront the physical reality that she had died here, looking at these miserable lights, my mind would only relate it to myself. I caught myself wondering despicably if I had crossed her thoughts during those last hours – as a memory or a regret. The sheer egoism of that unnerved me; in one of my books I would have called it a schizoid response. I kicked up a loose stone and turned back to the group. The worst deaths always begin by making you feel embarrassed.

Chapter Twelve

As he drove me back to town, Whitaker managed to slip in a little interrogation. The preliminary softening-up was masterly. He had stopped to light a pipe.

'Thought you might like to have a look at these,' he remarked, as he pushed a large brown envelope at me before returning to the business at hand. I removed the large glossy photographs carefully, expecting blown-up snapshots of Johanna when she was alive. Nothing could have prepared me for what I saw.

It looked like a jigsaw puzzle for trainee butchers.

There was nothing human or intimate or individual about her left. It was just meat. One of the incisions had scooped out a sodden trough between the legs. Muscle and intestine and skin tissue erupted over most of the torso. In at least two places actual bone pushed its way out with maniacal dedication.

But the worst madness of all had been reserved for the head. Not that you could tell it was a head. The face, for one thing, was no longer actually there. It had been pulped, leaving a broad livid gap for the mouth. Even the eyes were gelatinous shreds hanging off the skin.

I had to put my hand to my mouth to stop myself retching. I was remembering Poe's horrifying story *Berenice* in which the narrator's obsession drives him to cut out the dead heroine's teeth.

Whitaker was monitoring my reaction discreetly. When I started winding down the window, he was solicitous.

'Yes they're not too nice. If you'd like a little air?'

I stood outside for a minute, leaning on the car. I was not going to give him the pleasure of seeing me vomit, but I didn't want to talk.

I found myself refusing to accept that the mad intestinal diagram in the pictures was Johanna. All the lost emotion I had been repressing throughout the past forty-eight hours pushed to the surface.

And it conspired to find a way out: she was unrecognisable, therefore she was not Johanna. That was my one slender hope and I clung to it.

When I felt sufficiently composed to get back in, Whitaker did not start the engine.

'There's no rush,' he said kindly. 'You might as well have a few more minutes to get yourself together.'

And then he began asking me questions.

Even at the time I knew he was deliberately exploiting my shock. He asked about my movements over the past weeks both in Weston and London. My work. The people I knew. And then back to Johanna. I was relatively guarded. At the time I didn't see how he could find any of the things I told him very interesting.

When we finally drove back to town I felt exhausted. But I did arrange to see Johanna's things the following day. Whitaker easily guessed the way my mind was working. 'I know she's unrecognisable but the identification is certain,' he said gently. 'There are her clothes, not just the ones by the road but some more by the body, and some personal things with matching prints on them. The pathologist may not have much but he has enough.'

He dropped me off in the town centre. Back in my room I lay on the bed in a semi-stupor, trying to recompose Johanna's picture in my mind, trying to see her as a human being again rather than a grotesque conglomeration of organs. I found it difficult. Whitaker's atrocity photos had bitten deep into my unconconscious.

I thought with relief about the other photo. I reached over eagerly to the pocket of my other shirt where I had left it, wanting to refill my memory.

Too eagerly perhaps, because it had gone.

Chapter Thirteen

After a lot of futile searching I gave in. Like an idiot I had forgotten to carry it with me. Nothing else was missing.

I even began to wonder if the whole briefing with Whitaker had been arranged just so the photo could be removed.

But why would anyone care that much about a comparatively bad photograph of Johanna? I was certain it contained no hidden visual clues. There were no other people in the picture, the background was blurred. In every respect it was unremarkable. Later, after a few drinks, I rang the police to ask if they had released a picture. I was told they were hoping to issue a photo supplied by the girl's university within the next twenty-four hours, there were no others they knew anything about. I had ransacked my room a dozen more times, before I finally collapsed into bed.

The following morning in the catacomb-like basement of the murder building I was led down some steps to a room which smelt chemical and unpleasant, like a public lavatory.

Behind a desk, indistinct metal shelves stretched obscurely away, and after a few moments, some black polythene bags were thrust in front of me.

They looked dark and inhuman, bulging sealskin peelings. I was almost reluctant to touch.

'It's all right,' said the young policeman beside me. 'All the lab tests have been done on these.'

I picked up the first one and opened it. Inside was a Shetland sweater with a patterned neck. I held it by the arms. It didn't evoke anything. Below were jeans and a jacket in smart corduroy. So far, it was anonymous.

As the second bag was opened and I took out the Moroccan leather shoulder bag, I experienced a flash of time sickness. I could remember choosing it uncertainly in a Kensington boutique. Usually it had been overstuffed to the breaking point. Now it was empty. I paused a moment, the young policeman noticed.

'Recognise it?' he said.

'Yes,' I said. There didn't seem much point in dissembling. Another bag had underwear and the Egyptian-style wallet I'd been half expecting. It contained a driving license, an NHS card, some Tampax and a cinema ticket stub.

I examined each article. Even the signature on the license brought back unwanted memories. There seemed no more to be done. I was trying not to think of Whitaker's photographs.

At the top of the stairs I asked if I could use a bathroom. The toilet area was empty and I had recovered some of my equilibrium by the time the two men strode in.

I recognised one of them at once in the mirror. A solidly built, podgy-faced man of about sixty, he was Jim Weatherspoon, a backbench Labour MP. I had once interviewed him at length about some pro-abortion legislation. Now his face looked tense and rather flushed. The younger man beside him in a neat dark suit wore a fixed smile.

I delayed in front of the mirror, because I wanted to know what Weatherspoon was doing there and it seemed more fruitful to eavesdrop than interrupt. To my regret they urinated in silence, but I sensed a definite hostility between them.

As they were leaving, something unexpected happened. Weatherspoon stopped dead as if he'd made up his mind about something and turned to the other man. 'It'll have to be raised,' he muttered. 'I'm going to raise the whole matter.' The other man said nothing, and they left.

The open air was a relief after the police enclave. I decided to take another look at the murder site and when I reached the nearest spot to the copse, there was only one other car out there besides a police car. Evidently the story was already losing its news-value.

Up at the clump of trees where she was killed, a reporter was talking to the two duty policemen. If the killer had dragged Jo there, he must have parked his car here at the bottom, then dragged her uphill by the most direct route. This was evidently how the police saw it. I examined around the side of the fence. The weather was now warmer but any trace would probably have been erased long before by rain and frost.

I squeezed through the fence and walked up towards the copse of trees and the three figures. As I approached, one of the policemen nodded. The journalist was conducting a formal interview with the more senior of the two. He was from Birmingham, judging by his accent.

It was now a clear day and I stood a little apart from the group, uneasily aware of the unoccupied policeman's eyes on my back. I stared at the land sloping away from me and wandered ineffectually along the crest of the hill. It seemed useless, and I wasn't keen for them to see me snooping around. Finally I returned to the policemen as the reporter, head-down in the wind that blew along the edge of the hill, trudged back down the slope to his car.

'Any clues then?' I asked rather feebly.

'We were going to ask you that, sir'.

'No,' I explained, 'I'm just getting some more atmosphere for my story. No leads?'

'There are always some leads,' said the senior officer looking at me with the sort of hostile expression that passes for neutrality in policemen.

'But nothing definite?' I persisted.

He shrugged in reply. I turned back to the car and he shouted after me. 'Will you be staying here, sir?'

'Yes,' I looked round with a contrived smile.

When I got back to the car, I drove back along the track to the proper road. It occurred to me that they might just be mistaken about the path the killer had taken.

Suppose he hadn't parked in the safety of the lane at all, but had stopped on the nearest spot along the main road to the copse of trees and then struck off uphill. Of course it made the police even stupider to have missed him on the night. But it would hardly be the first time a police investigation had missed something so obvious. He could have dumped her up at the copse, and returned to his car and used any of the farm roads as a way home.

I drove slowly back along the route to the town, keeping a bearing on the hill outline, with the copse of trees just visible in the distance beyond. Some way along and only about three quarters of a mile from the copse, a field path led up beside a small beech wood and then petered out. There was just room for a car. I turned and drove down, with a

51

hedge on one side and beeches on the other. Then I got out of the car and walked back to the road.

But to my disappointment, the car was clearly visible to anyone who passed. Even so, I reasoned that the murderer might still have parked there briefly. And if he was in a Land Rover he might even have been able to hold this almost non-existent track until he joined the farm paths further across. That way he could have dragged Jo up to the copse and then disappeared without going back to the road.

I got out and checked for tyre-tracks. But a closer examination of the field-track revealed that even a good Land Rover would find it impossible. The undergrowth was too thick.

I walked on through the trees until they thinned out into a single line of beeches, on a short strip of grass. At the end of the strip, a primitive stile gave way to the slanting fields which would eventually lead back up to the copse.

The trees offered the grass some protection from the elements, and it was well-trodden. Possibly the police had explored here but I wasn't sure. If the murderer had come this way, it made their search on the night of the murder look even more ludicrous than it seemed already.

I walked along the strip, as far as the stile. My first inspection revealed nothing but then I noticed some dislodged grass and exposed earth. There were no animals nearby. It dimly occurred to me that someone could have taken advantage of the fence to struggle.

I looked more closely at the ground around the marks. A tiny bit of dirty whiteness, half-embedded in mud was buried by the post of the fence.

I bent down and dug into the mud. The thing was fairly far under which suggested it had been there a few days. Pulling it out, I realised it was a bit of paper screwed up tight.

For some reason, before unfolding it, I glanced nervously over my shoulder at the fields stretching above and below. There was no-one around. The wind blew lightly through the beeches on one side.

I unscrewed the paper fold by fold. At first it was impossible to see for the mud. There was printing. I scraped the earth away with my finger.

A supercilious scornful face stared up at me. The face of

Wellington. Above that another face, a face drawn by me: two eyes, a nose and a smiling mouth.

It was the shredded filthy remnant of the five pound note I had given to Marie on Christmas night.

In that split second I knew that Jo might still be alive. Then I saw the danger.

PART TWO

FEAR

Chapter One

I don't know how long I crouched there by the fence, staring at my own dilapidated artwork. It can't have been more than a few moments, but in that time everything changed.

I felt like a botanist who had gone out for an interesting stroll among the flora and fauna of his own garden and suddenly finds himself in the middle of a jungle.

By her own testimony, and the police's testimony, Marie had set out for Birmingham in a police car carrying this thing. Pretty close to the time of the murder. And now she'd disappeared and it turns up here, covered in what looked like little splashes of blood, and a completely depersonalised corpse lay in the morgue alongside a load of personal identification.

You could read that a million ways but the first thing it suggested was that the police account of Marie's movements on the night was fiction. Somehow Marie figured in the murder, perhaps as the victim. And the police drama department version in which a lone maniac regrettably disposes of the town whore was beginning to look increasingly like a tacky melodrama for public consumption,

Then I had a worse thought. Perhaps I was meant to find these ominous little clues which led nowhere? Whoever lay behind all this, they would have little trouble in setting me up. The session in the basement that morning may not have been for my benefit at all – my fingerprints were now all over Johanna's documents. Suddenly I could see the evidence against me clicking into place like a row of jackpot nines on a slot machine. A long and secretive liaison with the deceased, a sudden drive from London on the night of her death without explanation or alibi, followed by furtive and highly suspicious behaviour.

And what did I have to support my speculation? The disappearance of a runaway hitchhiker and an old five pound note with my own writing on it. The mysterious photograph had already vanished.

A branch creaked and I looked around, half-expecting Whitaker to step out of the trees and arrest me, trying to dispose of incriminating evidence.

I got back to the car and carefully placed the note in a compartment in my wallet. For a long time I just sat there, agonising over the choice between the motorway and my possessions in the hotel. Finally, after persuading myself that I could telephone the hotel from London with a convincing excuse, I turned towards the motorway.

When I reached the roundabout above the various feed roads, I looked down from it to check the southbound entrance. A white police Range Rover stood guard directly below me on the hard shoulder. If I was stopped and identified now, I'd have lost everything. No amount of explanation could make up for the abandoned belongings and unpaid hotel bill. The police below me might just be a routine patrol but I wasn't prepared to bank on it. My only feasible alternative was the meandering B-road by which I'd first arrived. It doubled back slightly before reconnecting with the motorway about 40 miles south. But if they were keeping an eye on the motorway here, then they wouldn't neglect this other approach. And, as I circled the roundabout, I could just make out a stationary black car at the foot of the hill. That didn't prove anything but it made up my mind.

It was getting dark as I approached the hotel and parked the car with some care down a side-street facing west. At the hotel reception I feigned a cold and asked for a half-bottle of Scotch from the bar.

The girl went away for a little, possibly to consult her father, but she came back with a bottle of Teachers. I paid her for it by cheque and then walked up the stairs, coughing loudly.

In my room I sat in semi-darkness until my eyes became adjusted to the light. After taking a swig or two from the bottle, I remained completely still, oddly encouraged by the thought that if the room was bugged, there was nothing in this darkened space for them to see or hear.

I packed my small case as quietly as I could, making sure nothing was left. When I was satisfied, I lay back on the bed and wondered whether it was worth trying to rest. Finally, I decided it would be safe to shut my eyes. I knew sleep wouldn't come.

A vision of Johanna kept returning. Not dead or threatened, not even neurotic and real, but tactile and statuesque. Her head bent forward to look at a book, eyes large in absorption, hand on cheek. Loops of hair falling in her face. Lips wide. Like a child gazing into a rockpool. The image made me want to weep. But I couldn't.

Chapter Two

Around one am I swallowed five amphetamines.

The face of a friend of mine still flashed through my brain whenever I swalled them: bones through drained flesh; one evening her tooth crumbled against a glass.

But speed is unfairly denigrated on account of its addicts. Amphetamine is only the physical equivalent of an overdraft. Temporarily it improves your performance in everything except sleep and sex. You just have to pay back the energy debt and, if you don't, the resources give out.

I had written a cheque out to the hotel for an amount I could calculate from the daily tariff behind the door. Now I scribbled a polite note, making my excuses.

Outside in the corridor there was neither light nor sound. Like any small hotel, this one went to bed early, but as I plunged down the stairs into the blackness, these last few steps seemed the worst part of the whole plan. I kept expecting a dozen people to jump out at me.

Crossing the hall, I raised my hand to the bolt, which was about two thirds of the way up the heavy oak door. I found it and slid it back as slowly as I could.

It grated sharply. The sound of metal against wood echoed through the house. I stood there waiting but nothing happened.

Turning the handle, I pulled gently but it still held. I tugged again and noticed it was holding lower down.

There was another bolt at the bottom. I wished the speed would begin to hit me, this was clumsier than an eighteenth-century elopement. The second bolt slid easily and I swung the door open.

There was nothing outside but a couple of parked cars on the other side of the road. The wind seemed icy but it hadn't frozen. I closed the door gently and checked the hotel windows, which were all dark.

Sliding quickly along the side wall, where the streetlighting was engulfed by shadows, the street was soon visible both ways. There was no police car or patrol in evidence.

I had been quite prepared to find one waiting. Perhaps this time tomorrow I would be in my London flat, laughing at my own paranoid imaginings. Then I thought of the thing in the morgue.

The streetlights through the trees made crazy patterns on the pavement like the ink blots in primitive psychological tests. Every square stone seemed to suggest something heavy and emotional: a battle, a death, an accident. I crossed quickly to the side road and the car.

Its dark squatness loomed unobtrusively out of the night. I put my bag on the passenger seat and sat inside, taking a deep breath. The speed was beginning to take effect and I could feel it easing into my head and muscles in a warm gentle flow. A part of me could relax and plan while something else took over my body-controls. Like the autopilot in a difficult plane landing.

I turned the key and the engine fired.

My route would take me along the only exit road I hadn't already seen. The toll-bridge to the north-east was hopeless. I could remember it from my visit with Jo, all these years ago, slow and conspicuous with a high proportion of lorries. The way I'd arrived wasn't any more appealing for obvious reasons. Nor was the murder road.

Even if I could have negotiated the farm tracks the motor-way roundabout could not be avoided. That left a B-road running west out of the town into underpopulated Shropshire hill-country. Much further on, it crossed into Wales. But I could turn off before that and double-back at a suitable distance from the Weston area to hit the motorway well south.

I gathered speed tentatively and moved through the silent streets, getting slight palpitations from the drug. The route I had planned took me along the quieter suburban roads and I saw no other cars. As I went up the hill through a tree-lined street, one lonely house was lit, but it looked like a burglar precaution. There was no other sign of activity.

The road went on climbing until the houses began to thin out and a few fields appeared between them. The slope was now downhill and I turned into the exit route. This was near the boundary of the town and, knowing it was more likely to be watched, I deliberately began to increase speed past the chemical works and what looked like a small army base. The speed-limit sign finally flashed past.

Fields still alternated with the houses and the ground got flatter, the speed was sharpening my responses, warning me that this straight was potentially dangerous, an obvious place for surveillance.

My hands held the wheel lightly but tensely. The car crossed an intersection, then another. I was certain that the houses would end just ahead and my spirits soared.

There was now open countryside on my left. Another intersection was threading past on the right when I caught the streak of light.

The robot-reaction, induced by the speed, brought the steering wheel down hard left with terrifying abruptness as the blue Cortina darted viciously out of the side road. I caught a blur of a blue uniform in the driving seat and he was aiming his nose straight for my door.

The Mini spun to the left just in time and the impact, intended to kill me, caught the side of my rear bumper. The car swerved wildly, mounting low pavement and skidding back onto clear roadspace. I fought to regain control as the road slewed from side to side.

And then, like some kind of visible and audible miracle, the whole countryside opened up behind me in a blaze of lights and sirens.

It was less a threat than a revelation because it seemed to me then that the whole army of conspiratorial forces that I'd been shadow-boxing for the last week had been tempted out of their lair.

The speed pumped adrenalin through me, and the speed-robot drove in a measured frenzy as I stared with an almost spiritual wonder at the contorted riot of colour and sound in my rear mirror. Sirens and lights and engines rose together in an unholy unison.

There must have been at least four police cars waiting in a state of poised concealment in that side road, besides the unmarked Cortina. And there was now only a gap of about two hundred yards between me and the pack leaders. Their speed and power was enough to make the outcome of any car chase inevitable.

We were out of town, moving through precipitous open

country, full of bends and hillocks. The space between us narrowed and the sirens gradually muted as though they knew the issue was not in doubt. My eyes desperately raked the country on either side. A wood went by and the road came out of it on a series of sharp bends.

As I rounded one, my headlights picked out a stretch of unfenced park-land sloping upwards towards trees and separated from the road by a short precipitous slope. It was covered in medium-sized stones but it was the only chance I had. My pursuers were not yet round the last corner and, praying aloud, I braked sharply, clicked off my lights and freewheeled at about forty miles an hour over the edge.

I hit one of the bigger stones almost immediately, the right wheel banged upwards under me as it blew out, and the car tilted a few feet in the air, sending me crashing through my defunct seat-belt into the passenger door and clutching at the spare seat.

Then the wheels hit earth again and skidded on for another thirty yards as my shoulder painfully collided with the dashboard.

I pulled at the door which seemed immovable, dreading being trapped like an animal exhibit as my pursuers closed in.

But the robot revived enough to make me unwind the window and bring down the handle from the outside.

Grabbing the case beside me, I stumbled out onto the turf.

Up on the road things were confused. The leading cars had gone on but two pack followers must have heard me. They were out of their cars shouting, and one of them was reversing, either to put his headlights on my car or drive down after me. I didn't wait to find out which.

Running as low and as fast as I could, I had soon slipped across the field into the black sanctuary of the adjoining wood.

Chapter Three

All I could think about was getting as far away as possible. I stumbled against trees, light and shadow flickered before me until the wood was a picture show of moving shapes.

Even the pain from briars which scratched my legs and from my arm, which had been rebruised by the fall, scarcely registered. It must have been ten minutes before I dragged myself straight into a pile of deadwood and sprawled forward amongst the crackling spiky branches, still clutching foolishly at my bag.

I lay there listening to the sound of my own breath, feeling a little blood run down my left leg. Gradually the thinking process resurrected itself.

I tried to take stock. A mad dash across the landscape would be the swiftest route back to the Weston police. No matter how fast I moved, I couldn't outpace them. But the trail I made could be followed by a sleepwalker. It would also attract the attention of all the surrounding countryside.

I lay there absorbing as much as I could. The wood ran uphill in thick lines in a westerly direction and the slope upwards had not eased my frantic progress.

It was just thick enough to deaden sound, so the quietness around me didn't necessarily mean my pursuers had given up. If I moved along the side of the hill I might be able to reach the perimeter of the trees and see what was happening. It was vital to get a proper perspective on the surrounding countryside. Otherwise I was caught in a box which could be nailed down very quickly.

Fortunately, out of the wind it was not cold for a winter's night. Picking my way between the trees and branches took longer than I had hoped, but eventually it led to a space, through which I could see a lighter patch of black.

I crawled forward and peered out. Compared to the pitch dark of the wood, the field that now spread out in front of me was well defined. Straight ahead I could see a stretch of open space and, in the distance, more trees.

To the right back down the hill was not so reassuring. Only about half a mile away was a line of torches.

The sound of occasional shouting and the yelping of dogs floated over the east wind. They were moving slowly and I guessed I was looking at the only visible part of a cordon which extended through the wood below me.

I marvelled at the efficiency. It was not more than twenty-five minutes since I left the car and already my trail had been marked down.

If the wood was being cordoned I had to think very fast. They were moving slowly but they knew the ground and I didn't. I could run on, but for all I knew, what was spread out below might only be the beaters of the shooting party, forcing me into the arms of the guns ahead. Their radio contact must have been excellent or this whole operation would have been impossible.

My mind raced. I considered a dash across the field into the trees. The cordon couldn't be that wide. But I didn't want to risk showing myself, especially when I had no way of knowing how long the cordon was. By the time I got over there they would be dangerously close, and the flank might come round at me when I could least handle it.

That left the worst option of all, which was to try and get through them. The more I thought about it, the more intelligent and the less attractive it seemed.

The main problem was the dogs.

I got up and retraced my footsteps back to the pile of deadwood which had ended my mad dash. Close by was a large old tree with copious thick branches. It looked like the kind of tree a panicky city-dweller would choose for refuge. After looking closely at the trees beside it and seeing one I could climb, I embraced the first tree crazily, hugging arms and legs around the base making sure that sweat and blood ran into the bark. Then I took an old shirt from my bag and began to climb the tree as slowly and clumsily as I could. At the top I mopped my face and arms with my shirt and hung it to the branch.

Back on the ground I hacked a path from the tree as destructively and indelicately as I could. If the wood had not been so deadening, the noise would have brought them to me in no time. Periodically I lay on the ground, rubbing my face and hands against the leaves, letting what sweat I could pour onto them. At times I urinated. The process was slow and demoralising but I knew the wood didn't extend too far.

I was just beginning to lose my nerve when the trees ended abruptly in a wire fence. A wooden gate loomed nearby and I opened it as wide as I could. The yapping of dogs still sounded far away on the wind. They were doing the job thoroughly. Running into the ploughed fields I made about fifty yards and then stopped.

The ground below me was not frozen . The soil came away in my hands without too much difficulty. Soon there was a medium-sized hole for my case. I fumbled it open and took out jeans and another pullover.

I ripped off my soaking and bloody clothes and changed, naked and shivering in the field. I transferred my money and pills, stuffed my old clothes back into the bag which I covered with earth. It might just waste a little precious time while they dug it up.

The moon had pushed out from behind its cloud lair, bathing the whole scene in a faint but iridescent glow. It must have looked like something from Robert Louis Stevenson, a macabre disposal of treasure by moonlight.

Now came the most agonising part. Step by step I retraced my own tracks back across the field. Twice I nearly screamed with frustration when I couldn't at first see where to put the next foothold; each time it finally appeared at some unlikely angle. Only once in a blind panic, I was forced to turn my back on the wood and move backwards towards it, making new tracks.

After what seemed an eternity I stepped through the open gate on tiptoe and there in the moonlight I noticed a squat rectangular structure a short distance along the fence. After a swift calculation I abandoned my track and tiptoed over to it. To my delight it was a long low cattle trough, still two-thirds full of water. Up to this point I had been trying not to think too hard about my progress, but this was a possible bonus.

Dropping my spare sweater and gritting my teeth against the agony of cold, I clambered over into the water and submerged.

It was pure iced pain. I forced my head completely under. Then I floundered out onto the grass.

I was contorted with cold and pain and it was hard to resist the temptation to dry myself or pull on the dry sweater. I staggered back in the direction of my track, feeling sick and dizzy but the sounds were clearer now. The dogs would soon be at the tree.

Perhaps it was fortunate that I was too weak to run very fast back along the trail towards the tree I had climbed because the noise might have alerted them at once. I made a slow semi-silent lollop, dripping with water, trying to make as little impact on the vegetation as I could. It seemed numbly suicidal to be heading straight into the arms of my pursuers.

After a while I could hear their sounds becoming louder. Yaps from the dogs, the rapping of branches and occasional shouts. But still I couldn't see the tree I had climbed. Vainly gathering speed, my foot caught a root and I sprawled onto the ground.

For the second time that night I lay impotently under the trees, but now the wood floor trembled and echoed with the noises of my pursuers.

I just lay there, eyes tightly closed, smelling leaves and wood. Momentarily I mimicked the childhood superstition that if you can't see your enemies, they can't see you. And then I imagined the dark shapes picking their way through the trees, until they silently encircled this glade and my limp defeated form.

Quaking with cold and fear, I got up and saw that a faint glimmer of torches was already visible. Silently imploring the speed-robot to regain control, I tiptoed along the trail. Even at this moment I could still feel it somewhere inside me, the architect of this whole catastrophic plan.

Then I saw my tree, and alongside it the chosen refuge – a tall sapling with a number of thin but firm branches, which overhung the track I had made.

Summoning all my last reserves, I raised my hands and pulled myself as delicately as I could onto the first branch. Then, abandoning all caution in the immediate necessity of concealment, I pulled myself up another branch.

I climbed once more by this method and then it was necessary to use the trunk. Soon I was relatively high in the crook of the tree, surrounded by branches, but even the denser thickets below me couldn't conceal the beams of light which were encroaching like a line of fireflies.

A sudden increase in noise from the dogs soon announced the discovery of the first tree. There were answering shouts from the men and I expected to see lights converging.

But to my dismay the line held rock steady. That meant none of them were going to break formation without news of a definite sighting.

The next fifteen minutes stretched on interminably. It was vital to my scheme that the first tree should hold them for a while but soon I began to wish they'd move towards me. The other enemy, cold, was beginning to get inside me. My whole body was icing over.

In one sense it had been madness to plunge myself in the water. I gulped another two tabs of speed, and washed them down with the Teachers, which miraculously remained intact. Perhaps it would help to keep the circulation going.

Below me, the discipline of the searchers was amazing. All of the motionless torches were pointing forward, presumably to provide a clear line of light in case I suddenly broke cover. Perhaps they had already seen me and were simply waiting to move in on all sides.

There was a shout and the torches swung downwards, the line was beginning to move again. I waited. The slightest sound would be lethal. I could sense the presence of people below and hear the panting and sniffing of dogs.

My trail was attracting the maximum concentration of men and dogs. The entire wood seemed to shift under their feet. I could even see outlines of men in the shafts of light and caught one brief flicker of a face, attentive and excited, before the beam crossed back to the ground.

Then everything collapsed.

A dog stopped below the tree, barking wildly and scraping at the trunk. Others were racing on, presumably, as I'd planned towards the smell of sweat and urine. But someone had stopped below me.

'Another tree,' shouted a voice, and a powerful beam snaked up through the branches. It just penetrated the fork where I lay, sending little pincers of light directly onto my leg.

A voice from in front shouted: 'Max do you want us to hold the line?'

And the first voice answered: 'Yes I do.' It was a deep authoritative voice with a local accent.

I heard the line stopping a few yards past the tree. The dogs were almost uncontrollable. They had reached the main part of the sweat run. My chief hope, and it hadn't worked.

Two beams swept the tree from top to bottom. And then to my horror the sound of creaking wood and a muffled oath.

Someone had climbed onto the lower branch.

I felt utterly helpless. The sound of heavy breathing came from only a few feet below me.

The light snaked up again, narrowly missing my face.

Then the other voice called back, 'Max this trail's fresh. Let's get going, we've already wasted time.'

Nothing.

Then a thump as something hit the ground.

Max's answering voice was a little surly, 'Well the dog don't mistake unless it's deliberate. These trees're deliberate.'

But he was back on the ground.

There was a shout and to the other dog's delight, the torches began moving forward again. The noise receded until it seemed as though I was alone. I couldn't be sure that one of them hadn't stayed behind just in case.

I sat there, waiting.

Chapter Four

Finally I was convinced. Even in my cold and cramp, the speed helped to give me a sense of exhilaration at winning this much of the round. It was delicious to pull on the other sweater after all the exposure. I estimated a half an hour at least before they picked up my trail again, and they might not even manage that.

I crept back down the tree and made my way across the wood.

Out in the open, the lights were only barely visible. They were converging on my clothes, which was good news. Even better, a thick lair of clouds swamped the moon and the night had turned much darker. Two drops of rain lightly hit my head as I surveyed the scene.

I welcomed the rain despite the prospect of a completely unprotected hike across country. It was the one thing that would obscure my trail completely.

The grass field dipped into a furrow that allowed me to move fast and offered good cover. After some judicious scouting, I celebrated the rain with a sprint to the edge of the field. This exercise was the first thing to make my body feel human again. I was only strong enough to do it because of the speed, but the warmth it granted was genuine and not synthetic.

Since the cordon was heading west, I intended to move southwards skirting the town and then find somewhere to sleep before daybreak. If I could make five miles or so, that would see me out of immediate danger, and I might be able to hitch a lift to London. Across the next field a stretch of farm-track headed in roughly the direction I wanted.

For the next three miles I made reasonable progress, passing two farms, both dark and undisturbed. The speed-robot was pumping my arms along callously and, though the results were good, I was already dreading the feeling that would hit me when its influence began to wane. I could not go on using the stuff indefinitely or the physical backlash would be unbearable.

First light found me crossing a kind of low moorland. The speed had almost worn off and I felt deathly. Cold ate into my hands and feet, and my head was torn by a vicious headache. The only choice lay between sleeping and taking more pills.

Looking back in the direction I had come, a line of low hills cut off the town from view. This was scrappy farming country.

I was climbing a gentle grass slope, when I saw the ragged outline of figures ahead of me. I dropped down listlessly. No movement. I advanced.

It turned out the figures were dressed in shredded black tweed and bits of sack. A moth-eaten assembly of scarecrows. They seemed to be guarding a small stagnant pond.

When I got closer, I couldn't work out whether they were there to protect the water or what was growing around it, but there was no-one about.

A farmhouse was just visible half a mile north. Behind the pond was an old wall bordering a clump of trees which would afford some protection from the wind. And the scarecrows offered warmth. Dismantling the biggest one, I slung the dry heavy rags over me and found a relatively sheltered patch on the other side of the wall.

Covering my head with the smelly remnant of what had once been a shawl, I felt more secure. And I fell instantly into a fitful and unpleasant sleep.

I dreamed about a black dog driving me up a tree to shouts of amusement from faceless onlookers. His breath was frostbitten and every time he got close to me, I could feel little crystals of ice condense agonisingly on my skin.

Then he began to cough and scream, and I woke up frozen and feverish to a noise that sounded like a dozen tractors.

A shiny helicopter hovered over the scarecrows like some giant insect. For what seemed like hours I crouched where I was as the noise of the engine hung directly above. I thought it had seen me. But, circling around the hill, it finally roared off to the north, gaining height.

I peered back over the wall, but there was no sign of anyone. It was already late afternoon.

I was impressed, and more than a little dismayed, by their

ability to bring in a helicopter. But the Commission were notoriously efficient. It was how they got such good results.

When I finally summoned up the courage to lumber out from behind the wall, I half expected to see a field army advancing over the hills to meet me.

The incident determined my next move. With a silent apology to my poor overworked metabolism, I swallowed six more Dexedrines and set off as rapidly as I could in the southerly direction I had been travelling.

The countryside soon gave way to more farms and fields and minor roads but it was mainly open land. As the tablets hit for the third time in fifteen hours, the robot dragged my exhausted mind and body from its stupor and I became more adept at dodging through gulleys and making use of the available cover.

There were not many people on the land this winter afternoon or I would probably have attracted attention. Once I was nearly seen by a farmer strolling through a kale field with his dog, but I got down just in time. The dog barked a few times until he was called to heel.

By the time the drug's effect had peaked, I had encountered a promising road running south and slightly east. There was an excellent chance it would connect with another town or perhaps a motorway roundabout from which I could hitch. I stayed close to the hedge, occasionally jumping for shelter when a car approached. Fortunately the road was empty enough to enable good progress without detection.

And eventually the roar of distant traffic became audible. Soon I could see a gash on the darkening landscape and a BP trailer flashed momentarily into sight.

I had actually hit the motorway much earlier than I expected so I hadn't travelled as far as I thought. I suppose I should have been elated but new problems began to loom.

It soon became obvious there was no access road to the motorway. This was a drastic piece of bad luck, not just because it made hitching impossible, but because it could be miles to the next junction or service point. Looking down at the shifting grey line from the bridge, I felt like a mariner wrecked on a stormy and hostile sea, just a few hundred yards from a busy shipping route.

I walked on until the ground levelled off and then jumped over the fence into the patchwork of fields that lay along the far side of the motorway. My only consolation was that in the growing darkness I would scarcely be visible from the motorway itself, provided I stayed in the fields alongside.

But it was almost impossible to match the motorway's line. I walked through ditches and over fences, even crawling under a massive pipeline. I wondered who would have walked along these deserted fields before me. Farmers must tend them but fields beside motorways are like a world apart. You never seem to see a farm labourer there or even a tractor.

My diet of pills, unrelieved exposure and unremitting tension began to make my thoughts wander. I started mockbowing at the lights that sped past. Screaming at their noise. Once I found myself on all fours.

I was shouting into the wind when the mirage loomed up ahead of me, a red and white mirage which spanned the motorway like a colossus.

I was almost beyond caring, although I dimly knew that the letters 'TOP RANK SERVICES' meant something important. At last I took in the service forecourt, a pedestrian from another planet.

Chapter Five

The first task was to get to the men's room to clean up without attracting attention. Fortunately there were few people around because it was late, and the motorways carried far less traffic than they used to.

In the harsh light and heavenly warmth of the white-tiled toilets I examined the alien in the mirror.

His jeans were torn and covered in mud past the knee, and his long face was unshaven and glassily pale under dirt. The inner eyes looked like red sand. There were a few scratches on his hands and head, but they turned out to be not too bad once I'd cleared the blood.

I took off my shoes and socks and ran the wash-basin warm. Then I put one leg in it, letting the warm water disperse the worst of the mud and following the same procedure with the other leg.

It would be better to look wet than muddy. In the mirror the alien could just pass for some mechanic who'd been cleaning his car and got soaked, or perhaps an exhausted motorist who'd had to hitch back after a breakdown. I splashed my face with incredible warm water as I was letting the jeans and shoes dry.

Then I prepared to re-enter the world of humans. The forecourt was still empty but a giggling couple came out of the cafeteria. The girl had black curly hair and the boy had his arm round her neck, whispering to her. They didn't give me a second glance, probably because they were so concerned with each other. But it gave me the confidence I needed.

The cafeteria was ingeniously plastic, red seats and green ceiling with *Some Enchanted Evening* droning from half-concealed speakers. I stood in line and a few people at the tables looked round automatically but they returned to what they were doing. The waitress who poured out my coffee, smiled kindly and asked if I was hitching.

74

'Yes, caught the rain badly,' I said smiling back. The role seemed to play; I was pleased. I started to devise a more detailed version for later.

There were evening papers on the rack and I paid for one with the coffee. At a table, overlooking the kinetic sculpture of headlights below, I opened it.

The headline was a relief. 'Local Rates Blast Off'. So I hadn't made the front page. I flicked through it quickly.

On the inside front cover a photo jumped out at me. It was a photo of Jim Weatherspoon, the MP I'd seen in the toilet of the building which was CURV's murder H.Q. But beside him, inset, was another picture which staggered me far more, because it was unmistakably a picture of my own wrecked Mini in the field.

'Search for MP's Hit and Run Killer' screamed the headline. My name was right at the front of the story.

For a moment I could hardly believe the input of my own brain. In a series of rapid mental convulsions I actually wondered whether I had collided with Weatherspoon's car and was suffering from amnesia.

My fingers tightened around the coffee cup. I could feel the tugging in my head as it began to descend from the speed-induced high.

I read the story twice: I was wanted in connection with a fatal accident on the road from Weston to Sawsley late last night. 'The victim was Jim Weatherspoon, the well-known Labour MP, who died instantly when his blue Cortina went off the road.'

'According to an eye-witness, the Mini was being driven dangerously, and shortly afterwards its driver crashed into a field and fled on foot.' The rest of the story was a short biography of Weatherspoon.

I thought of the Cortina, which had lurched across the road, with a police driver who seemed bent on killing me.

I was beginning to feel like a team-player who has avoided the most ingenious pincer movement only to discover that he never had the ball in the first place. Even my most desperate manoeuvres against Weston were like stabs with a feather. Hit-and-run was a good deal more persuasive than a murder charge. They had the car and my clothes.

I racked my brains to recall Weatherspoon's exact words in the toilet of the murder H.Q. the previous day. He was

75

angry, and he had said he would have 'to raise the whole matter'. Raise what? Something to do with the murder investigation. And now they were calmly trying to take out both of us.

I swallowed my coffee, though it burnt my tongue and left the cafeteria. The faster I got away from the motorway the better.

I deserved some luck and it came. After only a few minutes on the exit road, a lorry pulled out of the service-point and the driver, who looked friendly, yelled across at me to get in. He was going to London.

I sat numbed and exhausted in the darkness of the cab. After only a few minutes we were passed in the outer lane by two police cars. The timing was perfect. I watched the lights flicker past as my host talked happily about his taste in rock music.

Through the twin independent agencies of luck and Dexedrine, I had got through their cordon. But Weatherspoon hadn't. I remembered his honest indignant face. As I fell asleep, its features grew red and gross and the mouth began to speak short obscentities.

There was a logic to them but, although I strained to listen, I couldn't understand what he was trying to say.

Chapter Six

When the lorry driver nudged me awake, it was morning outside. The north circular was sleek and wet. He looked at me intently without shifting his foot from the accelerator. 'You all right, mate?' his eyes were half-amused as though he'd been watching me sleeping.

I stared at him uncomprehendingly. Then jerked into attention, my senses still blurred and painful. 'Yeah, I was dreaming.'

'You were pretty tired,' he said. 'You'd only been in here five minutes when you keeled over.'

I looked out uncomfortably at the road, searching for a convenient tube station. But my head was beating like a drum. I had a speed hang-over, the worst kind.

I put my hand up to my forehead to wipe the sweat, it was hot in the cab and the engine roared like demons. My hand shook badly as it got up there. And the lorry driver was still eyeing me.

'You look terrible,' he said cheerfully. 'My old lady lives up in Tottenham. Come and have some breakfast, and a sleep. I pulled over after picking you up but I could use some more myself. I don't have to get this load in till tonight.'

I shook my head in protest, the last thing I wanted at this stage was to get caught in some compulsive hospitality. But my refusal came out sounding like weak politeness.

'You won't get anywhere like that,' he said firmly. 'You'll have a cup of tea at least.'

The matter was evidently settled, he wasn't going to stop. I felt too tired and ill to do anything about it, even if he'd proposed driving me straight round to the nearest police station.

It was a terrible way to hit London. A wash at his place might at least make me less conspicuous. I forced myself to try and concentrate on the details around me.

77

The driver was young with close-cropped hair and pasty skin. His face was small and bullet-like but he had a wide friendly grin.

The tiny cab was stuffed with tatty colour pin-ups. I wondered if his old lady would correspond to these dreams or turn out to be a prim little housewife. Probably the latter.

But I was wrong. Not for the first time in the whole business I forgot to take account of the distorting power of male fantasy and male projection.

We pulled up at a grey terraced house in a side street off Tottenham High Street. The fresh air revived me a little. He let me into a small living room and, after putting a kettle on in the adjoining kitchen, he offered me a seat and pushed over a packet of chocolate biscuits. I took one and ate it hungrily, staring at my surroundings.

The room was an odd mixture of punk and chintz. The colour scheme was pink and brown and there were mallard ducks hovering on the wall. But Sid Vicious stared out from a wall-poster and an ancient juke box squatted under the ducks. He saw me looking at the juke box, and went over to plug it in.

'D'you know Winston Churchill's on RCA?' he said.

I frowned as he raised a finger and pressed one of the selection buttons. Eventually a 45 flipped onto the turntable and a familiar gruff voice came out of the speaker.

'We have become the sole champions now in arms to defend the world cause,' it said. 'We shall do our best to be worthy of this high honour. We shall defend our island home and with the British Empire we shall fight on unconquerable. . . .'

'June 17th,' said my host grinning. 'After the fall of France. They just released all his old BBC stuff on EPs.'

The effect of the voice in that setting was hearteningly incongruous. It turned out that the lorry-driver, whose name was Leslie, had two heroes: one was Elvis and the other was Winston and they were both on RCA. He was treating me to further selections from the two of them when the door opened and his wife came in.

Everything about her seemed to emulate the same sexuality that was indulged in her husband's pin-ups. I guessed she was only about twenty-three but her hair was bleached blonde and pink hoop earrings hung from her lobes. The skirt and blouse she was wearing were several sizes too tight, and her legs perched perilously on high and shiny heels.

'This is Rhonda,' said the lorry-driver, carefully approving her appearance. Rhonda smiled as though she was being shown off and asked if I wanted sugar.

The tea was scalding hot and reviving. And as I sat there making conversation, I found that the sight of Rhonda's tarty 50s-style uniform had reawakened uneasy memories. Memories of the salesman's lecherous description of Jo and her exaggerated behaviour. Rhonda's outfit was acceptable enough here – a self-conscious and eccentric archaism which fitted, in a crazy way, with her husband's taste in records. But in a place as sexually stifled as Weston it would seem violently out of place. Sexually subversive even. Like a porno film at a prayer meeting.

I ate the chop and potatoes they offered me with little-disguised greed. The food eased my headache and I explained to Leslie I'd be grateful for a few hours sleep on the sofa and the chance to use their phone. Shortly afterwards they disappeared upstairs.

I called John at the paper not only because I knew I could trust him, but also because he would be the best possible ally. We agreed to meet at his flat at five and I spent the rest of the morning and most of the afternoon in dreamless exhausted sleep on the sofa.

Later I debated whether to leave money for Leslie and Rhonda but decided they'd find it insulting. Outside the streets were wet and cold.

Chapter Seven

I had expected to feel a sense of release from the city, but instead it felt claustrophobic.

The old man on the tube opposite me stared rudely. I wanted to stare back but I knew that it wasn't worth the risk. I couldn't attract attention to myself in any way. Instead I stared mournfully at the floor, reassuring myself with the thought that no-one I knew was likely to be travelling at this time. It was only four o'clock which meant I had to fill an hour before reaching the safety of John's flat.

I think it was the homing instinct, amidst all the hostility that I felt or imagined around me, that now pushed me into an act of critical stupidity. My flat is off the Tottenham Court Road and the tube from Tottenham runs straight through Warren Street. I decided to chance seeing if the flat was being watched.

I was lured by the idea that in the city, unlike the country, you at least know where your enemies are. But I was wrong. The town is more like a treacherous sea. You can be lured by false securities, and thrown miles off course by misdirected panic.

It was totally mistaken to assume that a busy main road by a central station would afford protection. Nowhere can provide cover when you don't know what is safe and what isn't. The bus you jump onto may hold your real pursuers. The meths-drinker may have water in his ancient green bottle. The city, even more than the country, can be a land of illusion.

I came up the busy Warren Street escalator and out onto the street with relief, seeing a mass of people already trying to get home. The swirling crowds reminded me of all the familiar thoughts and emotions that seemed to have got lost in the last few insane days since Christmas.

If I had been thinking more clearly, perhaps if the speed-

80

robot had been at the controls instead of languishing somewhere in the back-oblivion of my brain, then that ebbing
mass would have had all the attractiveness of a coiled python.

But I walked out into it and let it carry me along. Behind
me a smart young couple with briefcases, laughed about
something. A woman in front walked hand in hand with her
little girl, an old man was looking downcast as if he'd just
lost some money at the betting shop across the road. Filthy
coat dragging, he turned disconsolately to examine some rubbish. And three men were shouting at each other about
football.

I was only about ten yards from the corner of my street as
the crowd in front waited for the pedestrian lights to change.
I intended to keep straight on going, but give the road by my
flat a good casual glance. When I crossed in front of it, I
don't know what I expected to see. Probably a man in the
street, surreptitiously pretending to read a newspaper.

Instead it all happened quickly. And there was nothing
subtle about it; the insanity I had been living for the last
week was suddenly and immaculately transferred to a rush-
hour street in the centre of London.

I didn't even need to turn my head. Three police cars were
visible as I crossed the street, two immediately outside my
flat and a third at the other end of the road. It looked like a
siege area, but there was no cordon and little public curiosity.

As I flinched instinctively, something hard came into contact with the small of my back. A woman's voice said, 'Police.
Go towards the flat.'

I turned sideways and I caught a glimpse of the smiling
young couple. They were still smiling as if I were an old
friend they'd just met in the street.

The woman had a coat on her arm covering the gun,
pressed against my back, in what must have looked like a
friendly hug. A hug that could shatter my spine.

I have never been in a similiar position before. But in that
moment of ice, when I realised that my spine could be cut by
a bullet, I had time to grasp that, whatever was going on, it
was still being kept undercover; they didn't seem to want to
arrest me in public. And that was my only chance.

I collapsed.

Or at least it began as a collapse and ended as a fast duck.
It was a futile action, originating more out of a refusal to

move than agility, and the barrel of the gun followed me down.

But as the couple's attention transferred downwards and they came to a halt, the people behind them on the pavement naturally pushed forward and I launched myself backwards at the woman's legs.

She could easily have killed me. The gun, still largely encased in its coat-muffler, pointed straight at my head. But a gaping bullet hole in full public view must have been a last resort when the victim was unarmed and on the ground.

Instead she brought the metal barrel viciously and inconspicuously down against my skull.

From behind it must have looked as though she was solicitiously bending down to help me after my fall. I could still see that wide-eyes smile looming over me as I took the impact.

It was above my left ear and I felt a sharp numbing heat down my whole back.

But even as the thing hit me, the force of the oncoming crowd and my obstructing body had sent her over me. Almost as an animal reflex I managed a kick at her as I crawled away.

The man had been left behind in this burst of activity. He may have thought I had been shot when I first began falling, and seemed to be more concerned with the encroaching crowd.

Now he made a sudden lunge at me which must have looked strange to anyone observing the imaginary scenario of their friend's 'fall.' But I easily eluded him between the feet of a woman and child who could see perfectly well that I was hurt, and moved side with according briskness.

By all the averages, this low-level diversion should have caused chaos and confusion among the pedestrians. But, like all the other deceptive trappings of the city, crowds have a knack of clearing when you least want them to, and the space began to expand around me with alarming rapidity.

Staggering to my feet and, without looking round, I loped back towards the underground exit, between the startled commuters.

Behind me, a siren wailed into life. My only chance lay in luck and speed. With the gash in my head I was now too conspicuous to melt into any London scene.

I pounded into the underground station nearly colliding

with a woman selling sprigs of heather. The ticket hall was crammed with people, there were heavy queues at the windows and there was no time for the machines.

I hurdled the barrier without even checking the direction. There was a shout from the ticket collector, which I ignored. He wouldn't be able to chase me, and the police would know my direction from onlookers in any case.

I risked a glance back as I reached the bottom of the escalator. There were three blue uniforms at the top.

Everything now depended on the trains. Because there is not a chance that a suspicious civilian can elude the police on a tiny congested station platform for any length of time. Commuters are too stuffy and too curious to let it happen, they would simply hand me over like a pack of dogs.

When I reached the platform, there was a tube directly ahead of me with its doors poised open in a state of suspension. By jostling through the crowd, I squeezed through the nearest door but it directly faced the entrance.

And there I waited second by second as the guard refused to close the doors. If the police appeared now, they had me cold. I was squashed into a tiny space, literally feet from where they were due to emerge.

And still the doors refused to close.

The pressure of people in the carriage was so great that even the feeble evading action of turning round would involve backing onto the platform or blocking the doors.

Time was suspended like an enormous pendulum. Finally in childish desperation I closed my eyes.

Nothing.

I opened them again and there directly in front of me at the mouth of the entrance were the policemen. They were motionless, looking straight at me.

It was like a crazy tableau, both of us standing there trapped by the crowd. Then they saw me.

In the moment of recognition the doors started to close. One of the policemen lunged forward and another ran shouting to the guard to stop the train.

But if there is one abiding rule about the rush-hour underground, it is that once the doors close, the guard can become completely oblivious to anything and everything that is happening amongst the press of people on the platform. We began moving and I could see angry police faces shouting at the guard's carriage. And then outside was darkness.

The elderly woman hanging onto the strap next to me, looked in my direction nervously. 'Were they for you,' she said in awe.

'No,' I said, 'I thought they were for you.' But she remained suspicious.

It was only now that I looked to the destination. We were heading north on the Northern Line towards Euston and Camden Town. If the police were quick they might be able to board at the next stop, Euston. Given the timing involved it would mean remarkable efficiency, but I had to plan on a possible radio link with a car parked on the Euston Road outside the station.

They would still have to get down to the platform in order to get to me. And Euston intersects with the other branch of the Northern Line and Victoria Line. I could stay on board but I reckoned that Mornington Crescent or Camden Town would be pushing my luck. That stretch is quite long and would give them time to cover the platform.

But Euston was clear and I darted out of the train. The Victoria Line was approached by another escalator and a long connecting tunnel. This time I walked rather than ran. The hair on the side of my head felt sticky and matted but most of the blow's force had been lost in the woman's fall and it had already stopped bleeding.

I tried to think of a persona for myself, walking tired and dirty and slightly hurt through the underground. I decided I was a garage mechanic who had been hurt in a small accident and sent home by his boss.

There was no sign of the police. On the platform I waited up at the far end. This line was less congested and a train was signalled. A man beside me in a suit asked me the time, and I explained I didn't wear a watch. Then I realised he was staring at my head.

'It happened at the garage,' I said. 'The bloody jack slipped. Lucky to get away so light.'

He seemed satisfied. 'You should get home,' he said.

'That's where I'm going.'

The exchange increased my confidence. It gave me a role. By the time I got on the train, I was expanding the particulars of my new temporary existence: what my wife would say and how long the boss would let me have off.

The police would by now be on the other platform, but as the train moved off there was still no sign of them. Then it occurred to me that they might have gone undercover.

With this in mind I slipped out of the train at Victoria, walked along the platform and then jumped back on as the doors were closing. A woman leaving the platform looked at me, but no-one rejoined the train when I did.

It had never occurred to me what an ingenious labyrinth the London underground system is. I took the train all the way to Stockwell where I changed back to the Northern line. Some people got off there but no-one made the change with me. I was sure I had got away.

I left the tube at Waterloo where the ticket collector accepted my money without interest.

To my relief it was almost dark outside. I walked across the bridge to the embankment by the Festival Hall. I was aware that any judicious investigator would be able to pick up my trail as far as here. So now was the time for extra care. John lived in a flat overlooking the river about half a mile along, near to Blackfriars Bridge.

Skirting the busy stretch of riverside by the South Bank complex, I kept to side roads, carefully avoiding the bedraggled winos who loomed up occasionally. The river looked black and forbidding and rubbish spilled out of dustbins and litter baskets – signs of the continuing South London refuse strike.

My head was now hurting badly and it was a huge relief when I finally came within sight of the flat. The ramshackle building had been converted and there was an intercom system at the door. After lingering on the other side of the road, plucking up my courage, I finally slunk across and leaned on the bell.

A voice came out of the metal grille and I spoke my name with an odd sense of unfamiliarity. I looked down at myself and felt the stupidity and incongruity of the situation. What was I doing, filthy as a tramp and gashed around the head, ringing John Platt's doorbell?

Two flights of stairs up, and John came out grinning with a bottle in his hand.

His expression changed when he saw me.

85

I suppose in my subconscious I had been storing up for this moment of release, the sudden translation back to my normal world, wondering if it would ever come. Now, when I was there, it all felt dream-like and insubstantial. My head was throbbing. I could hardly speak.

'I fell under a woman,' I mumbled.

Chapter Eight

The next night was New Year's Eve.

After twenty-four hours rest my brain had thrown off its vicious speed hang-over and, as I began to feel human again, John listened to an account of my adventures. A pale intelligent man, about ten years older than me, in his early forties, he was currently living with a German girl called Margit who spoke English so badly that she rarely tried. Most of the time she reacted to attempts at conversation either with amusement or irritation depending on her mood or what she was reading. John seemed able to read her mind exactly which was probably why they got on, but I never quite decided whether she was his lodger or his lover.

After we had gone over and over the business with Weatherspoon and the evidence of the crumpled five pound note, John took pains to point out that, as far as the murders went, all I had at the moment was negative evidence. Marie could have exchanged the five pound note. And if there was some kind of conspiracy we still had no inkling of how or why.

'Let's accept,' he said quietly, leaning forward in his old armchair, 'that it is Marie in the morgue. You have to assume a pretty corrupt police force, which is easy, and a corrupt Home Office pathologist which is less easy. The vanished photo could have been surveillance. They wouldn't want that in the hands of the press. But you still haven't got the merest whisper of a motive. What conceivable interest can any of these women be to CURV or anyone else?'

'They were in the way,' I said.

'Of course,' John agreed, 'but when someone is in the way you get rid of them quietly and effectively, mafia-style. You don't commit the most public murders in England, nor do you swop one corpse with another like a game of musical slabs. Why take the risk? The body doesn't have to appear at all. The person can quietly disappear.'

'It's almost as if they wanted it to be as public as possible,' I muttered. But I couldn't explain that and we argued around the subject for a while without getting any further. John intended to make some enquiries among Weatherspoon's colleagues in the morning, and also arrange a chemical check on my five pound note. We celebrated the New Year with mixed feelings.

In the early hours of the morning my mind was exhausted and Margit disappeared to bed. We started talking of other things including our work and the sexology book I was currently supposed to be writing. John expressed curiosity about the seedy little scene I had witnessed behind the curtains in Weston on Christmas night; eventually I found myself asking if he had ever felt any ghost of incestuous desire himself.

He thought about it for a while: 'Maybe, but that isn't terribly dramatic,' he said. 'I mean most little boys and girls are supposed to dream of their parents carnally. But you adjust. Isn't that basic Freud? You abandon infantile desire for the parent in exchange for the promise of sex to come.'

'Yes that's an approximate paraphrase,' I said, 'but in researching the book I came across a question. Why should you? Why should any child bother to abandon it? Why doesn't the family just indulge itself?'

John thought for a minute. 'Because inbreeding would destroy the species. You end up with lots of deformities and freaks. Like the Hapsburg kings.'

'That isn't quite true,' I said. 'In fact some geneticists think inbreeding would actually benefit the population.'

He looked disbelieving. 'Yes,' I continued, 'others think it might do harm, most aren't sure. And even if it was harmful, how could early man have known that, when some tribes don't even appear to have realised that sex and babies were linked?'

'OK,' said John leaning back in his chair, 'but it's more sensible to assume that it is harmful and somehow we know that instinctively so we don't practice it.'

'But, if we knew it instinctively,' I said, 'why would there be laws against it? You don't have to pass laws to back up human instincts. You don't decree that people should eat or drink. Laws are only passed when society wants to *overcome* an instinct. To prevent people grabbing something that might be good for them but is bad for society.'

88

'Aren't there primitive societies that do practice incest?' John asked. 'It's just that the ones that ban it have got on better.'

'That's the fascinating thing,' I said. 'You can find almost every conceivable kind of social organisation and activity in the world or in history. Societies based on cannibalism, on the worship of animals, on legalised murder. But incest on a large scale is probably the rarest social phenomenon there is. It happened during the Roman occupation of Egypt in the first few centuries AD when marriage was legalised between brothers and sisters.

John shrugged, 'So brothers and sisters got married in ancient Egypt. That doesn't seem too relevant here and now.'

I pounced. The truth was it was fun to talk to John about a subject I knew better than him. There weren't many. 'OK but what about this? A few years ago an American social researcher who decided to look into this question unearthed *twenty* brother-sister pairs living together as happy and socially accepted married couples within a single American state.'

'With children?' he said.

'Not only with healthy children,' I said. 'One of the couples were apparently son and daughter of an earlier similarly incestuous mating. So none of this is quite as outlandish as it looks. There have always been rare isolated cases like the one in Weston. That's what makes the subject so interesting.'

There was silence in the room, broken only by a foghorn from the river. Eventually John spoke.

'Do incest and sex-crime ever go together?' he said. 'Could that be a possible link with the murders?'

I shook my head: 'No, almost never. Incest is all in the family. According to all the studies I've seen, you can't correlate incestuous fathers with murderers or rapists. The pattern is different.' My mind returned with reluctance to the subject of Weston. 'But I still don't think these were sex murders.'

John sensed he had me cornered and he was probably relieved to get me off my lecturing stool. 'Well if they weren't sexually motivated, what the hell *was* the role of sex in them then?' he said. 'I mean the first body was covered in semen. What else do you call it?'

I struggled to put my feelings into words. 'Well if sex had

anything to do with these crimes . . . then maybe it was a kind of victim.'

John roared with laughter. He had argued me into a blind alley. 'The ultimate Jack the Ripper,' he said. 'Making the town pure. But why?'

I stared into the fire, trying unsuccessfully to see a way through the labyrinth. I found myself thinking about the immediate future. We'd already arranged that I was going to try and sneak out of London via a night-sleeper the following night while John pursued various enquiries. He had a cottage on the east coast near Edinburgh I could use, and it seemed the safest place.

'But there is an important difference,' I said at last. 'Whoever he was, the first Jack the Ripper left scores of whores in Victorian London. This one has completed the job. If there *were* prostitutes in Weston, he left none at all. They were crucified.'

Even at the time the verb somehow seemed to hang there.

The following morning John came up with the most unobtrusive clothes he could find: dark brown sports jacket, brown polo neck, grey nylon trousers and Hush Puppies. It was a bit like going back to fourteen, especially since Margit had cut my hair that afternoon. In the mirror I looked like an underfed private, and there were plenty of those on the streets that winter.

Later I met John at a pre-arranged rendezvous at an Edgware Road cinema.

'OK,' he whispered as he sat down. 'I've got it. Booked you through to Aberdeen just in case someone traces the purchase later. He looked around to make sure we weren't disturbing anyone but the sound-track was loud and the nearest spectators were several rows away. The ticket passed between us.

'There's also some good news,' he went on. 'I've been in touch with a colleague of Weatherspoon's in the Commons. There are already several rumours surrounding his death.'

The noise of the sound-track dipped. John paused. He went on more quietly and succinctly. 'He wants me to run the whole story so he can follow it up with a question in the House.'

It was better than I could have hoped. After today I would

90

be reliant on public sources of information like John's own newspaper. There was no phone in the cottage and we would be contacting each other only in urgent circumstances. John still risked a criminal charge if my whereabouts were discovered.

From the screen a voice was screaming, 'Don't look at his eyes.' The film was a revival of an old black magic thriller.

In spite of all my mental preparation, as John left me, I now suffered a strange and nerve-racking desolation, the same panicky limbo feeling that hits you when you travel vast distances entirely alone. Afflicted by this mood, even the most trivial domestic activities of those you are leaving behind seem desperately desirable.

I thought of John, going back to his flat, doing some work before supper, going to bed early. The time went by agonisingly slowly. Finally, as the heroes were deftly piloting their car into the centre of a rather muted Satanist orgy, I got up and left the cinema.

Chapter Nine

I got off the bus on Euston Road a couple of blocks short of the station, making sure that no-one was following me.

I walked jauntily into Kings Cross, making for Platform 4 as directly as I could.

A couple of uniformed policemen were standing chatting cordially to a ticket inspector on the next platform. There was nothing unusual about this. In recent years, the main English exits to Scotland were more closely watched than they had ever been.

I kept my face turned away from them as I walked up to the ticket inspector. To my immense bad luck he turned out to be Scottish and friendly, 'All the way through, is it sir?' he said, clipping my ticket. 'Well you've got half an hour if you fancy a drink here. The train won't be off till half past.'

'I'll go on now,' I said offhandedly.

It was an idiotic misjudgement. Hostility always increases people's suspicions. I should at least have returned his smile, but I was acutely aware of the policemen so near at hand.

'Suit yourself,' he shrugged.

It was only a short exchange but I caught one of the policemen looking across at me.

Thirty yards down the platform, I risked a glance back.

Another crass error.

All three of them were staring after me. I tried to walk more slowly but I was so nervous my feet were racing.

By the time I boarded the train I was fully prepared for a hand on my shoulder, but the three of them were still there chatting at the barrier. Perhaps my luck was holding after all.

The sleeping-car attendant was a small rat-faced little man with a welcome air of disinterest. After he'd checked my ticket I told him I had had a long flight and didn't want to be disturbed before Aberdeen, an arrangement with which he seemed perfectly happy.

My sleeper looked out onto the platform. It was the standard compartment, the first one in the carriage as you walked down the corridor, with a neat little bunk, a folding-top basin and numerous hooks and inlets for storage. It smelt slightly of soap.

I put my small case obstinately on the floor, locked the door and then sat down on the bunk, raising the blind enough to see out onto the platform. There were a few more people coming onto the train now.

I lay back on the bunk and closed my eyes and waited. It took all my self-control.

After an age of banging doors and footsteps and laughter, the carriage made a first great lurch. And then we were moving.

I felt an anticipatory shiver of triumph as I got up to stare out of the window. Craning round I could just make out the ticket-gate, and the two dark figures of the policemen turning away.

I closed the blind and lay back fully-dressed, experiencing the nearest thing to pleasure I had felt all that day. There is always something hypnotic about a tiny bedroom being conveyed through the night at reckless speed from one country to another. Even in those hunted circumstances.

I watched the mug rattling above the basin and listened to the strange orchestra of noises from the wheels and rails below. I had no intention of going to sleep but as the carriage rocked its way through the night I was lulled into unconsciousness.

The stillness of the train was what woke me. It was so quiet that I wondered if we had broken down. But there were no raised voices. Eventually I clambered sleepily off the bed to open the blind.

By the light of a clear moon I was looking down from a grass embankment over dark fields.

My watch told me it was 12.30 which put us about two hours out of London, somewhere in the north Midlands.

A small alarm stirred. But I ignored it, anticipating the first jolt of movement from the wheels below me.

Instead, after a while, I could make out some indistinct sounds further up the carriage towards the engine.

I unlocked my door and slid it open.

The corridor was light and as I watched through the crack three men emerged from a compartment at the far end and tapped on the door of the next one down. Two of them were in police uniform.

I was completely trapped.

When I looked out again, they were already much closer.

I grabbed my case and slipped down to the end of the carriage.

There, I was confronted with two equally hopeless choices. To carry on down the train would be to walk into the arms of suspicious attendants and probably more police. Yet to leave the train was, in the long run, equally futile.

In the end, just to get out of their way I edged open the outside door on my sleeper's side.

There was no sign of police but it was dark and uninviting. I clambered down onto the track and abandoned my case in the grass. Then I moved stealthily along towards the engine.

Looking back now I can only suppose I was half-remembering my escape in the woods outside Weston, which had been achieved by getting past the police cordon. If so, it was a stupid mental analogy because the circumstances were so different.

The night was windy and it must have been raining because the earth was slippery underfoot. I had to keep well down in case anyone was looking out of the train. Eventually I gave up and crawled underneath a coupling to check the other side.

Only a little way along, the grassy embankment extended to join a coarse tarmac roadway, that served the railway maintenance crews; there was a little hut with a corrugated iron roof alongside it. Beside the hut was a police Panda car.

A solitary driver got out and kicked his feet, eyeing the train with impatience. He was young and he looked half awake.

It could only be a matter of seconds before they discovered my abandoned sleeper. He turned and got back into the car, and I wracked my brains for an idea. Finally my eyes settled on the corrugated iron roof of the hut.

I scrabbled around on the track for a handful of medium-size stones. Then I crouched down by the rails and took aim with a pathetically shaking hand.

The throw was pitiful.

Two of them barely travelled thirty feet, another skidded into the grass beside the police car. I had no more hope for the other.

But the wind saved me. It must have lifted the fourth stone which hit the roof with a tinny clatter.

The driver started out of his seat and ran shouting into the darkness behind the hut, pulling out a walkie-talkie as he did so.

I sprinted madly towards the car. It was parked sideways on the hill with the passenger door facing me. The driver didn't reappear but I could hear some activity back down the train. They must have arrived at the compartment.

To begin with my luck seemed unstoppable.

The passenger door was unlocked and, sprawling inside the Panda car, I felt the key in the ignition. With a lunge of triumph I twisted it hard, willing the engine to roar into life.

But some frivolous god in heaven had at that moment bored with my run of luck. Instead of the sound of the motor there was a sharp click and something came away in my hand.

Impotent groping soon revealed that the metal head had sheared off in the lock. In my frenzy I had turned the thing so hard against the grain that it had snapped.

I sobbed aloud in anger, scouring the ring for a replacement. But the ignition was effectively jammed.

There were shouts from two sides. The driver was yelling nearby while fainter cries sounded from the other direction. I was completely sealed in. But the car was on a steep slope and I could freewheel. I let the brake out.

Nothing happened.

The driver was very near now, on the edge of the tarmac itself. Suppressing a wave of panic, I opened the door and used my feet to push.

It was all that was needed. The Panda car began to move forward down the slope, swinging wildly to one side until I grabbed the wheel. And even as the driver reached the point where his car had been, I was gathering speed.

I turned the lights on and soon I was careering along the tarmac and preparing to manoeuvre the corner at the bottom.

My pursuers were only figures in the distance. To them it would look as if for the moment I had got clean away.

I took the corner uneasily, only just avoiding a bad tail

95

swing. But my spirits rose to see that the road continued steep and precipitous for another quarter-mile at least.

The speedometer needle climbed and it was harrowing trying to negotiate the bends. I allowed myself gentle braking on a particularly sharp corner. There was now no-one behind. A tarmac path fell away to the left and I took it, hoping to find some means of concealment for the car.

The road took a couple of sharp turns and then to my despair it began to climb. There were high banks on both sides.

My momentum just took me over the crest of the hill onto the flat, before the car ground to a sedate halt.

This was the worst of all possible endings. While I had the speed on the main road I could at least have got the car into a field. But here on this easily accessible drive it would only be a matter of minutes before discovery.

I pulled open the door and stood trembling on the country lane, listening and looking. I imagined the night drive back to Weston, surrounded by my captors, quietly triumphant. Or would something less civilised be arranged? They must be a little impatient, now that I had openly resisted arrest on at least three occasions.

the night was cold enough but the sweat poured down my inside arms, while my legs felt like ice.

Sick and terrified, I tried to listen for my pursuers. But all I heard was my nails scratching down the paintwork of the car.

The faint lasted only a few seconds, but it took me close to real panic. I got up and ran nowhere. It was only further along the lane that some semblance of organised thinking returned.

The slope on which the car was stuck, turned out to be long but relatively gentle, and it soon gave way to another corner. Around that, it became clear that this was the drive-way of a private house.

Finally, I came to a small elegant building with a circular forecourt. The upstairs curtains were drawn and there were no lights visible. A real dead-end. I thought of ringing the bell and appealing to the owner. Then I saw the neat twin-garages.

The first one housed a new-looking Mini. But the car was locked.

The second was dark and empty but after a moment's fumbling I discovered a torch on a shelf. Turning it on, I realised this was more of a glorified garden shed. Tools, a ladder and a hose, all hung neatly from the wall, and an old bicycle in the corner looked more like a memento than a means of transport. An oil heater, some petrol cans and a short length of lattice fence lay on the floor.

It took only a few moments of relatively noiseless activity to clear a space. If I could shove the car in here, that would take it out of the police's immediate view. Especially since they did not know the ignition was jammed and would be looking further afield.

I ran back down the drive. The car was still sitting where I had left it. I started pushing.

It moved about an inch.

I straightened the wheel, and tried again. This time it went forward but I had to strain to stop it from rolling back.

My hands were beginning to sweat. I kept imagining the contemptuous laughter as they rounded the corner to find me pushing their own car up a hill. After several feet of heavy exertion I had to jam on the handbrake.

I had hardly covered any ground at all. My resolution began to waver. I wanted to run, to get off the road. I was sure I could hear footsteps behind me.

I kept forcing myself to let off the handbrake just so as I would have to push the car to avoid losing ground. I shoved against the frame with both hands, my legs bent and my head bowed with effort.

I was making gradual but steady progress when my foot slipped. The car slid back, just missing my hand.

Getting up and rubbing my hands against the seat to force life back into them, I used my jacket for padding against the door-jamb in an effort to stop the sweat weakening my grip.

This time, as I pushed, I bit my lip until I could feel blood on my tongue.

I was ready to scream. But at last I felt it moving downhill.

The momentum of the slope was enough to take me along the straight and round the corner. The rest of the drive was downhill. I had a little difficulty angling the car for the garage but I finally pushed it in squint.

I was in the process of creeping back outside when my leg collided noisily and painfully with the oil heater. It clattered against the stone and I waited for the house-lights to come on.

But nothing happened. They must have been sound sleepers.

Outside the garage there was no noise at all. Either my pursuers had passed by, or they were waiting.

Chapter Ten

My only chance was to break across country in search of a hiding-place.

The land bordering the driveway was wet and slippery, but easily negotiable. I was not being followed. After a few hundred yards I came across a wire-mesh fence around a field of pasture that sloped away uphill.

The road was off to my left, effectively masked by trees, and I took the hill as fast as I could, slipping frequently, in order to put as much distance as possible between me and the house.

I was so disorientated that it was only when I came over the hill that I realised I was climbing back towards the railway line. The familiar grassy embankment loomed out of the dark landscape ahead of me.

My first reaction was horror but the fugitive instinct quickly reasoned that the best chance of escape was to cross it and head east. So I began to climb the fenced slope.

It was steeper than it appeared.

I was near the top and panting with exertion when the sound reached me: a long low blast not more than a few hundred yards to the north.

In astonishment I realised what it was. My train was still there, stranded uncertainly like an abandoned tanker in a fog. During the furore of my escape the police must have abandoned the train without telling the driver whether to go or stay. And now he was nervously signalling his departure to the surrounding countryside.

Once the possibility had presented itself, I regarded it as the occupant of a life-raft would regard an ocean-going liner. It was the one thing they might not suspect.

I pounded down the track in the direction of the noise. I tripped once on a sleeper and went reeling into the mud, but the train turned out to be nearer than I thought. Some blinds were raised as awakened sleepers attempted to discover the cause of the delay. Up at the other end the guard and some attendants were holding a shouted conversation with the driver.

I made for the first class carriages at the top of the train, gambling that some of them were empty. With an optimism based largely on wish-fulfilment, I felt sure they would not be searched again.

Beside my darkened sleeper I was amazed to see the clear outline of my bag a few feet down the embankment. This was a welcome sign that there had been no time for a proper search before the police disappeared after me. It seemed Weston had not known for certain that I was on the train, or they would have arrived with far more manpower. The police at Kings Cross must simply have communicated a suspected sighting.

Everything was quiet as I clambered up the step and peered into the empty corridor. Then after getting the door ajar, I went back for my bag. Fortunately there was no sign of an attendant and I guessed he was out having a conference with the others by the engine. Passing two compartments in the corridor for luck, I pulled at the door of a third.

A little boy in pyjamas was lying awake, staring out into the night. I shut the door before he could even look round, muttering an apology.

A knock at another door further down got a faint response and, fearing a confrontation in the corridor, I dived straight into the next sleeper and pitch darkness.

I had a lunatic story ready but the cubicle was empty and untouched.

I locked the door and checked that the blind was secure. After a few moments a door banged and I heard voices out in the corridor. It was probably the attendant returning.

I lay down on the bed, finding it impossible to relax, wondering what to do next. After a while the carriage gave a shudder.

As we began to roll, I tried to work out exactly where the train had stopped. The landscape outside meant nothing to me. But since I was sure there had been no long delays before this, it seemed likely we were not more than half an hour from Doncaster, the nearest stretch of the line to Weston. The question I had to face now was what was going to happen next.

My whole plan was based on the assumption that until they found the abandoned police car, all their efforts would be concentrated on that, and the train would recede into the background. After all, they had seen me leave it with their own eyes.

I washed and changed my clothes, which were covered in sweat and mud. With a sense of luxury, I took out a clean pair of jeans and a sweater and a jacket. Then I scraped the mud off my shoes. By the time I had finished I looked quite presentable again. I combed my hair in front of the mirror, and was pleased to note my hand had almost stopped shaking. I just had time to turn off the light and let the blind up a few inches before we started slowing down for Doncaster.

Chapter Eleven

At first, the platform looked deserted apart from the usual mail and goods handlers.

But, as I watched, a couple of uniformed policemen came onto the concourse, evidently summoned at the station-master's instructions. After a chat with the guard, they entered further up the train and much to my amusement they re-emerged a few moments later, carrying my coat. There was a little more conversation before they disappeared.

We started moving again. I lay in the darkness of the sleeper, telling myself that I had almost come through. There was no point in doing any more calculating, everything now depended on them and virtually nothing on me. Perhaps it would take them most of the night to regroup and I was sure that once the train had crossed the border, their task would be even more difficult.

In York, the platform was swarming with police, most of them in uniform. Three of them were only inches away from my head when the train stopped, and I had to lower the blind completely.

When I raised it again, most of the activity still centred around my abandoned compartment. The attendant was giving an enthusiastic statement. A few other uniformed policemen walked up and down the train, with that particular air of men who want to seem efficient but have no very clear idea what they are looking for.

The loading and unloading completed, most of the policemen withdrew, having satisfied their conscience. But two very obvious plainclothesmen still hovered around.

While the last doors were being closed, I watched with a sick feeling as they leapt smartly onto the train.

They might have come along just to keep an eye on things. Or to make a more detailed examination of the abandoned sleeper. I kept telling myself that. But all I was really doing was waiting for the handle to turn.

I sat there in the dark, staring at the door for about a quarter of an hour. There were no footsteps, but the more I thought about it the more certain I became that, if there was any search at all, maybe just the random search of two zealous Yorkshire policemen, an empty sleeper would be the first place they would look. This conviction rose into a kind of despairing certainty until I was almost prepared for the miserable humiliation of being found there.

For the millionth time I reminded myself there was nowhere else to hide on the train. The traditional fugitive always barges into the compartments of accommodating young women, but that particular fiction had always seemed stupid. The whole train was already alerted, there was no refuge.

Yet in the end, I got up defiantly. If they were going to search I would rather chance it in one of the toilets, where at least there was a remote possibility of bluff.

I put on the small light and looked at my case. With some judicious remaking of the bed it was possible to get it out of sight.

The corridor was empty when I opened the door. The train was going fast now and the carriage rocked violently from side to side.

I walked down to the toilet as confidently as I could.

There was still no-one about and it seemed worth checking the next carriage down. I pulled the sliding door carefully and stepped through it. The train threw me gently against the next toilet, and it swung open. Then I peered round the end of the corridor.

I saw him halfway down.

He was leaning back against the corridor rail, chewing something, his arms folded. As I watched, the other one came out of a sleeper and went straight into the next one, brandishing an identity card.

There was no politeness this time. They would kick the toilet door down if they had to.

The corridor one was lean and narcissistic. He actually smiled to himself as he chewed. Probably rather a fun assignment, looking at everyone in bed. Then he glanced up in my direction and I withdrew, palpitating quietly.

I was stunned. After all this, they were going to get me so easily.

I ran blindly back up the carriage. Reaching the connecting door at the end, I found to my horror that it was locked. This was the end of the train.

And my rail journey.

Behind me I heard the toilet door slam. They were getting closer. I couldn't even go back to my compartment.

Chapter Twelve

I stood there stupidly at the top of the corridor. Waiting for them to reach me. The armpits of the freshly-laundered sweater were already sodden.

Walls on two sides of me. The outside door on the other. And them behind me.

Like a rat in a cage, I tugged open the window on the outside door. There may have been some stupid idea of pulling the communication cord and jumping out, but I knew that would be worse than useless. It was a panic reaction.

I stared wildly out at the windswept landscape. As the driver braked for a series of bends, my attention was caught by the shining metal bar towards the engine.

It was cold and slippery to touch, but solid. The sound of another door slammed somewhere behind me.

I barely knew what I was doing when I removed the belt from my jeans and looped it through the bar, twisting it round and round my clenched fist.

The wind was shrieking at me to go back but the train's speed was slow enough. When I was sure the belt was really secure, I tried hauling my right leg over the sill, intending to sit on the window and then lower myself down to the ledge below.

But wind and fear kept pushing me back. I was straddling the sill, with my right leg out of the window, and my crutch was taking more and more of the strain.

I closed my eyes against the elements, telling myself I was tall enough to reach the step that I knew was just below the door.

The pressure on the top of my left leg was unbearable and the train started to gather a little speed but, like some pitiful Don Juan climbing onto a balcony, I couldn't bring myself to get the other leg over. I imagined being arrested in this posture of abject humiliation – a trussed chicken with one hand tied, and legs apart to urinate.

That was too much even for my cowardice. I pushed myself up, misjudging the momentum so completely that I might have left the window altogether, had it not been for the velocity of the wind. It pinned me, barely sitting on the edge with both legs dangling into oblivion and my hands clutching the bar.

I had only a momentary glimpse of the writhing shapes of trees and a rush of noise and cold, before I was slipping downwards and being twisted round towards the train. All the pressure was on my arms as I dangled terrified like a puppet in a cyclone.

I struggled pitifully to find the step with my feet. My hands twisted and stretched in agony but there was nothing solid below me.

Then as we rounded the bend I swung outwards from the train with a force which nearly broke my arms.

I screamed.

But the driver was braking again. As my body slammed back against the side of the carriage, my foot hit something which jutted out. It was the ledge.

I couldn't relax my grip but the pressure was off my shoulders.

The landscape shrieked by. I had only been there a few seconds but I couldn't last much longer. It was like being in a black wind tunnel. The pounding factory of oil and metal plunging through the darkness was awesome, and freak squalls burst from each object we passed.

The driver braked again but he had gone into this corner too fast, and the persistent jolting was so violent that I was choking back vomit. The strain forced my eyes open.

It was an almost religious moment.

The face of the chewing plainsclothesman loomed over me. His jaw moved rhythmically and there was a slight smile on his lips as he stared over my crouching figure at the landscape.

I watched, fascinated, not even daring to breathe. He raised his hands palms-upwards as if in supplication.

I didn't even realise what he was doing until I heard the window close.

106

Chapter Thirteen

Then he was gone. He hadn't even seen me.

The cold was penetrating. I made a pathetic effort to alter my position, to take some of the strain off my hands. But it was useless. I couldn't feel either of them except as vague sources of pain. The noise and vibration were overwhelming.

And soon I realised my fingers were slipping away from the bar like slowly waking animals.

A warm stream ran down my leg. I lacked even the energy to scream. All my will had disappeared with the closing of the window.

I tried to shut out the torrent of sound and pain in my head. But it was only so I could concentrate on a more positive emotion for dying.

When it came, the light seemed like part of a dream. Everywhere was flooded with stark white beams and I could see buildings and rails. For a moment I thought I was lying dead by the track and this was some mystical vision of a train ascending to heaven. But the backs of the houses were grubby and earthly.

The driver braked sharply and this time he kept on braking.

The loss of momentum helped the pain but very soon the whole train was so slow that I could have fallen off it. We were approaching a station or a red light.

I was so weak that even when we stopped dead and I was on the ground, I had to stick my hands in my mouth to get them warm enough to open the door. I bit each finger hard. They were icy cold, but at least I could feel the bites.

I twisted the handle round just as the train gave a jerk forward. The interior lay before me in three unbelievable dimensions. I collapsed inside, using my right hand to lever myself up to floor level. There was no sign of my two friends.

When I staggered down the corridor, finding novelty in the

107

act of walking, a woman in a dressing gown emerged only a short distance away from me. But she went in the other direction and disappeared into the toilet.

I blundered into the wrong compartment before I found mine, but the occupant must have thought it was just another police check. The third one that night. He didn't stir.

The bunk was as I had left it, my case untouched. I locked the door and crawled in, pulling the covers over my head.

We were well into Scotland by the time I regained consciousness and it was light outside. There had been no further search of the train. The plainclothesmen would have got off at Newcastle with little idea of how close they came to success.

I felt a quiet sense of triumph as I repaired the ravages of the night before in the mirror. My fingers had taken most of the punishment but they were not too conspicuous. Half an hour after we had crossed the Forth Road Bridge, as the train was approaching my destination, I slipped into the corridor. An attendant carrying a large bundle of dirty linen, showed no great interest in me, as I climbed out behind one other passenger and presented my ticket at the small dingy station.

The town had once been quite active as a port exporting coal to the Baltic countries. The remains of that period shrouded the decaying dockside close to the station, and the waters of the Firth looked gray and oily. The centre was just a few grimy streets, with the occasional shard of industry to remind you that it was on the fringe of the Fife coalfield.

The cottage was easily found. It stood about a mile out of town back along the coast, an austere granite two storey building. Looking at it, I wondered how I was going to endure a period of long isolation. But I need not have worried. They arrived on the third night.

PART 3

PENETRATION

Chapter One

It was the same day that John managed to break his story. *'Conspiracy Riddle Around MP's Death'* screamed the headline. I got back to the cottage and read the whole thing quickly without taking anything in. I moved into the kitchen, laid it out on the table and read it again, forcing myself to concentrate.

'Jim Weatherspoon,' it began, 'the backbench socialist MP, who recently met his death in the Midlands, may have been the victim of an organised conspiracy. This rumour shocked MPs on both sides of the House of Commons yesterday.

'Weatherspoon was discovered amidst the wreckage of his car in the early hours of the 29th December, a few miles outside Weston, Staffordshire.

The story referred tersely to the coroner's inquest for which I was still being sought as a witness, and the recent murder.

'It has now been revealed,' I could feel John hitting gear, 'that Weatherspoon may have been in the Midlands on a personal trouble-shooting mission in connection with the activities of the security-conscious CURV, and rumours of police corruption.

'Ten years ago he mounted a similar one-man probe into private security organisations on the Liverpool docks which resulted in five arrests and the suspension of a senior Liverpool police officer.

'The news of Weatherspoon's death last week brought sadness amongst MPs and a special Prime Ministerial tribute, but it was not until yesterday that these startling new facts came to light:

1. The missing journalist claims he saw Weatherspoon at CURV's Weston HQ only hours before his death, engaged in heated discussion with a senior official.

2. Weatherspoon's undamaged car was seen by the same

111

witness *being driven by a uniformed policeman* at the time of his alleged accident.

3. Shortly before his journey Weatherspoon informed a colleague that he thought he was 'onto something big in the Midlands.'

The piece ended with a short biography of Weatherspoon. And the inside middle of the paper was taken up with a more speculative and insinuating story about the murders under the heading 'Town of Tension.'

I suppose I should have been glad to see it all in black and white. Instead it left me depressed. There was so little that was new and nothing about the evidence I had found on the hillside or the missing photograph. A photo of Johanna had eventually been released by the police but it was far older than the one I had held so fleetingly.

My worst fears were confirmed later the same day by the BBC news interview I managed to pick up on the cottage's battered television.

As soon as I saw the sleek appealing features of Paines, the CURV officer from the Weston press conference, I knew beyond any shadow of doubt that he was one of them. Point by point he assassinated my story. The performance was a small masterpiece. Even when he accepted my facts, it was only to turn them round: a uniformed policeman was indeed, he said, driving the wrecked hulk of Weatherspoon's car as it was towed into town on the night of the accident. He had been overtaken dangerously by my Mini which later crashed into a field while attempting to evade the police.

That was just close enough to my version to make anyone doubt what I saw.

Paines went on to explain that the Mini's driver had been suspected of an involvement in Weatherspoon's accident, especially when he resisted arrest. But because of the lack of direct evidence it had been decided to let the charges drop.

At this point, he even had the nerve to express his sympathy for me. He said I was in a state of personal distress and he urged me to seek medical attention. It was all I could do to resist flinging a plate at the screen.

Obviously impressed, the interviewer asked him about other suggestions in the newspaper story. Paines replied with worried seriousness that if they were based on anything at all then he begged someone to come forward and substantiate them. CURV's brief liaison with the Staffordshire police, far from being a long-term operation of a sinister nature, was almost at an end and their files would soon be opened to reporters. It was understood that Weatherspoon had made a perfectly cordial visit there on the day of his death.

'So far as we can make out,' Paines spoke with feeling in a slow cultured voice with a soft northern inflexion, 'this morning's story is entirely based on the paranoid fantasies of a self-styled fugitive. And to use the death of a much-loved MP as the basis for such blatantly opportunistic muckraking is an insult to everyone who knew him.'

An item followed about two farmers who had discovered Weatherspoon in his crashed car. I believed their story. It would have been easy to arrange: his brakes could have been fixed or his corpse dumped in the wreck. No doubt there would be enough alcohol around for the coroner to blame drunken driving.

But the sheer bravado of the official explanation shattered me as it must have shattered John. We were right back where we started.

Later in the day, Weatherspoon's widow made a public appeal for her husband to be allowed to lie in peace. The inquest would satisfy her, she said, and she certainly had no faith in the gutter journalism of a newspaper that had consistently attacked her husband's views while he was alive.

I couldn't blame her. John was an enlightened reporter but his paper was a right wing tabloid and she evidently saw this as a last, vicious kick at a man when he was down.

Everything had conspired to outmanoeuvre us. I began to realise that it was futile to rely on the slam-bang techniques of investigative journalism. Police corruption and switched corpses are not much use as press fodder when you don't have the faintest idea of a motive.

That night I was lying in bed unable to sleep when the noises began from downstairs. Then a light shone blindingly in my eyes.

The effect was so aggressive that, despite my terror, I would have been out of the bed to defend myself. But the switch behind the door snapped on and the room was flooded with light.

A squat round-faced man in police uniform stood over me, two other men were by the door.

'How the shit did you get in?' I managed, willing him to stop studying me so intently. His mouth showed a lot of white teeth but he wasn't smiling.

He held up a key, and I started round to look for mine. It was still lying on the bedside table beside me.

'Only a duplicate,' he explained patiently. 'The local conveyancer was perfectly happy to let us have it in the performance of our duties.' He glanced at his watch. 'I meant to join you all earlier. My plane to Turnhouse was delayed.'

'How long have your men been spying on me?' I tried to sound indignant but I knew I was beaten.

'Two days,' he replied. 'Once we realised you had got back on the train it didn't take long. We'd appreciate it now if you'd come back with us.'

'Come back where?' I knew the answer.

'To Weston,' he said matter-of-factly. 'Statement.'

I lay there looking at him. It was the lamest story I'd ever heard. I was no longer under suspicion according to the news, and now they were dragging me off gestapo-style in the early hours of the morning.

'Why now?' I asked, trying not to show my fear.

'It can wait till morning,' he shrugged. 'But we'll just have to wait here with you. We have instructions not to let you out of our sight till these formalities are cleared.'

He paused and stared out of the window: 'It's very quiet here,' he said.

The point was effective. I could hardly be in a more vulnerable position than I was already. Even a moving car presented more possibilities of escape or alarm than the bedroom of a desolate and apparently surrounded house.

I kept reassuring myself that Weston would not want to risk suspicion by my disappearance now. Unfortunately the rationalisation did nothing to stop my heart banging.

The journey was like being shut up with three corpses.

The toothy uniformed policeman was in the front passenger seat, staring ahead. I shared the back with a swarthy plainclothesman. He behaved as if I wasn't there.

When I asked them to stop at a phone-box, they refused.

Any attempts I made at conversation met with blanket

silence. Once or twice the man in front of me conversed in whispers with the bald-headed driver. Otherwise, they were completely mute.

Despite all attempts to reassure myself, I was terrified from the moment that I got into the car.

I kept expecting the driver to make a turn onto some little woodland track where they could do it without any fear of interruption. Or perhaps the man beside me would shove a silenced gun against my chest. Was he averting his eyes because he didn't want to see his victim's face? The lights of other cars flashed incessantly against my retina as the engine droned on.

At dawn, we reached the motorway. I should have realised by then that nothing was going to happen on the journey, but it was still impossible to avoid panic. No behavioural psychologist has ever come up with a better instrument of terror than the night arrest. It gives the persecutor direct access to his victim's unconscious. At the end, I was just sitting there, huddled and withdrawn, willing the journey to go on for ever.

There was little room left for any emotional response when the gloomy suburbs of Weston began to filter past in the grey light of morning. I dimly noticed that snow was turning to slush all around the little houses.

Chapter Two

As it turned out, the threat implicit in the journey was a piece of total deception. Their tactics had changed. Illusion was now once again to be substituted for force. And Weston was an ordinary town again.

Whether I believed the illusion did not greatly matter. It was bound to demoralise me and I could not prove its falseness. The sole purpose of the journey's veiled menace was to soften me up for the banalities which followed.

I did not even recognise the murder building when we stopped outside it. There were no guards on the door, no passes. Inside, a porter in his shirt-sleeves was listening to the radio and some men were making a business of hauling a filing cabinet down a flight of stairs.

As if on cue, the demeanour of my escorts shifted. Clumsy jokes were cracked, coffee was provided and a call was put through to John on my behalf. They even apologised for being poor travelling companions.

This Jekyll and Hyde transformation, like the transformation of the murder building itself, had a ghastly familiarity about it. It was, as before, a version of reality which differed totally from my perception of what had actually happened. But this time I was too weak to resist it.

The question-and-answer session was a farce. It couldn't have taken more than about forty minutes and it concentrated with an exclusivity amounting to brilliance on non-controversial areas. When exactly did I see Weatherspoon? Had I known him before? Was I sure of the time I passed his car? Could there have been any indication that he had been drinking?

One policeman asked, the other wrote. When they informed me cordially that was all, I just sat there.

But it was not quite all.

'Your car's been fixed,' said the small policeman. 'We like

116

to stay on the right side of the press, but you'll have to get the keys from upstairs. I think he wants to see you.'

It was only outside when they were giving me directions that I realised 'he' was Paines.

I walked dumbly up two flights, wishing I'd managed to sleep in the car. Workmen seemed to be everywhere. The whole building was full of cheerful banging and whistling. Another stage-set.

The door to his temporary office at the top of the building was wide open.

Paines was on the phone, as I came in, but he smiled very pleasantly at me. He looked spruce and healthy. There was no hint in that fresh face with its bright blue eyes that he held down a demanding desk-job. His clothes were as smart and well-fitting as they had been at the press conference but less formal. The shirt was bright and open at the collar.

'Yes,' he was saying into the telephone, 'I would be very happy if you could.'

In my groggy state I tried hard to scrutinise him. The length of his upper lip gave his mouth a mildly voluptuous quality. But it was the only treacherous feature on a sharp and intelligent face.

He replaced the receiver and rose to greet me: 'I expect you'll be glad to see these,' he said, cheerfully, handing me the car-keys.

I took the key-ring without replying.

He sat down indicating a chair opposite his desk. My knees were trembling but I did not sit down. I was certain the night-ride had been a preparation for this and I wasn't going to allow Paines the satisfaction of seeing how successful it had been. I remained standing.

His smile gave way to a look of concern. He got to his feet and went over to stare silently out of the window at the street below.

'You know you're one of the people on my conscience,' he muttered with what sounded like real emotion.

I don't know what I had been expecting but not this. The teacher addressing an erring pupil.

I was suddenly conscious of the contrast between us. I stood before him in filthy clothes. Ragged, skeletal and exhausted. He was composed and concerned. I felt like a savage confronting a priest.

117

He turned and focused on me, his eyes wrinkled with concern: 'Your allegations against us are being investigated of course. I know how easy it is to get a false idea of the police. We make mistakes. People do get caught in the middle. Like you did.'

'I didn't get caught,' I said simply. 'Otherwise I'd be dead.'

He sighed, sat back down at his desk and cupped his hands under his chin, eyeing me thoughtfully.

'You're wrong about that. But even if you weren't . . . innocent people have got hurt before now in the pursuit of justice,' he said sadly. 'With things as they are in this country how do you expect it to be otherwise?'

'For what?' I said, following his gaze out of the window to the industrial wasteland outside. 'For a place like this with an invisible curfew all night, every night?'

He deliberated on that for a moment. 'Very arrogant and very patronizing,' he said finally. 'Do you have any idea just how successful this town has been in keeping crime off its streets? The crime rate here is actually falling. Substantially. For the first time since the early fifties we're winning the battle. You'd rather see all that reversed for some tourist colour?'

'From what I've seen of this town,' I said, 'I think I'd feel safer in Belfast.'

He leaned forward slightly: 'The callousness of you social theorists staggers me,' he said quietly. 'Like Kullen you'd rather see a society corresponding to your vague idea of normality – riddled with corruption and violence – than a sane, safe, healthy community. Well you'll have difficulty persuading the people who've been raped or beaten up or mugged.'

'Who's Kullen?' I said.

He ignored the question. 'Look, as I said, your allegations are being investigated. We're taking them very seriously. But some matters are very difficult to pursue unless we have evidence . . . I'm only a policeman.'

At that moment it occurred to me that just about the last thing in the world he looked like was a policeman. The dark blue pleading eyes. The winning smile. If I had just come into that room I would have taken him for a shrewd lawyer or a senior civil servant.

'Why did you drag me here?'

118

Paines looked at me keenly. 'You came here of your own free will I hope?'

I was too angry to answer. I wished I had not been scared into coming willingly. Without a few bruises to show, the police's behaviour could even now be made to look innocuous.

'You see,' he went on carefully, 'I was hopeful some of your suspicions would disappear now that we've reached some conclusion.'

'What conclusion?' I said contemptuously. 'Have you decided it was all just hide-and-seek? You still have a few mutilated bodies to explain away.'

'We don't think so,' he said quietly. 'We are already holding someone who will be charged at some point today.'

A little shiver went down my spine. I turned round, half-expecting Whitaker to step out from behind the door with handcuffs.

'Who?' I said.

'I'm afraid I can't reveal that,' said Paines getting up. 'But you could still scoop every other reporter in London with what I've just told you. Perhaps we owe you that much.'

He actually came forward to shake hands with me, smelling of sweet aftershave. I stood there, disbelievingly, tempted almost to spit in his face.

But then, just for a second, the pupils of his eyes met mine and I noticed two things. The first was that they were dilated, though the light in the room was normal. Rounder and bigger than they should have been.

And they also held an emotion that completely belied the smooth facility of his posture and expression.

It wasn't deep loathing, which I might have expected. Or even rage. It was negation.

The look of a perfectly behaved child who finds it convenient to suppress a lethal pool of will.

I don't think it was intended for my benefit, but it scared me enough to make me stand there mute. He shrugged and let his hand drop, still smiling.

When I finally got down to the street, the Mini was waiting primly outside the murder building. I had virtually destroyed it piece by piece before I was convinced that it was safe to drive.

119

Chapter Three

The accused turned out to be a dim-witted welder, with a van, called Chris Wright who lived two villages away and had a long history of sexual offences. These predictable details didn't come out till much later but I think I could almost have recited them as soon as I knew an arrest was imminent. Whatever the nature of Wright's involvement, I was sure of one thing. He had as little to do with what lay behind these murders as I did. Probably even less.

I felt dulled as I drove away after the interview. Paines had all the jarring generosity of someone who knows he's on the winning side. There was nothing he wouldn't do for you; even to the extent of indulging you in his own sense of righteousness. In some ways I preferred his previous tactics.

I drove south, crossing over the motorway and put three villages between myself and Weston. After swallowing a dull two course lunch in a roadside hotel, I lingered over the coffee, trying to regain some energy and mental clarity, and thinking about the name Paines had let slip: Kullen. It meant nothing.

Around five as the light faded, I headed back towards the town. I was determined to have one last look. It had occurred to me to re-investigate the old abandoned pub on what had once been the village main street.

The High Street was deserted and breaking in through the rotted shutters turned out to be a simple operation. In the dim orange light filtering through the window the main lounge looked haphazardly gutted; the floor was thick with dirt and vermin droppings.

The derelict bottles behind the filthy bar were fly-blown and empty, non-returnables left over from some last wake. But on a shelf half-way up, tucked behind the empties and a decrepit advertising board, I came upon a relatively virginal

120

miniature of brandy, and drank a silent toast to the germs on Paines's body.

The alcohol went down well and, in the hope of finding some other cache, I slid my hand along the shelf under the bar. It was inches deep in dirt. There were no glasses or bottles, but I felt something small and metallic. The dim light from the street revealed an old Yale key, probably a spare for the front door. I slipped it into my pocket just in case.

Upstairs I discovered an old candle and some matches on one of the mantelpieces but the rooms were depressingly empty. The whole place had a haunted feel about it, it smelt of decay and poverty.

I was about to go back down when the candle's light picked out a door on the upstairs landing that I hadn't noticed. It was smaller than the others, more like a cupboard, and gave onto a steep and narrow bank of steps.

A dim flickering web of shadows spiralled around the filthy wall as I moved up the narrow staircase. There was a little more light at the top and it smelt different from the rest of the place, sweet and stale.

I raised my candle to survey the attic's interior.

An old bedframe took up most of the space. A rough wooden wardrobe stood in the corner. This was not surprising. None of the furniture would have been worth removing. The room was dusty and desolate. But closer inspection revealed that the floor was less filthy than downstairs. I wondered if a tramp had used it. There was nothing of interest except the wardrobe. I gave the door a quick tug and to my surprise it was locked. For the first time, I felt a pulse of excitement.

But when I took both hands the door came easily and I realised it had only been stiff. A couple of old hangers on a rail, that was all.

I was about to give up in disgust when I caught sight of a dark shape on the floor, hardly visible in the black recess of the cupboard. I had to bring the candle down before I could see it properly. It was easy to understand how the police had missed it.

A large black canvas hold-all. This time it really was locked, and there was no possibility of opening it without a knife.

Then I remembered the Yale in my pocket. It turned easily.

I delved inside it, and my hand met something soft and flimsy, which I laid on the bed.

In the flickering glow I could just make out a pair of black-nylon panties with a broad deliberate slash where the crotch should have been. I stared at it.

Then I pulled another piece of clothing from the tangled web and came up with an absurd uplift bra with round protruding holes for the nipples.

The harder shapes inside the parcels were shoes: two pairs of shiny five inch stilettos. Followed by more skirts and blouses, and a mound of exotic underwear, all in the same antique whorehouse style.

With my hand shaking so much that the light from the candle quivered madly, I went round the room a second time just to make sure there was nothing else. But no-one had lived here. It was a storehouse.

The moon came out from behind the winter clouds, throwing grey-white beams of light on the numbingly incongruous mound of lingerie. The moonlight added a strangely lonely resonance to the textures and surfaces. They looked like the costumes of some long-forgotten celebration. Dreamstuff.

The photographs of Johanna's carcass on the hill kept flashing on and off in my mind. In a futile attempt to break the spell, I tried to imagine the clothing inhabited by living and breathing female figures. But it seemed incredible that in another world this was the stuff of sexual desire. Because all I saw was death.

Outside a car went slowly past and I brought the candle down to floor level. A suspender belt gleamed. Then the engine died away. The interruption broke my trance. I piled the clothes back into the bag, and carried it downstairs.

At the bottom of the attic staircase I blew out the candle and returned it to the mantelpiece. There didn't seem much point in shutting the little door but I did it all the same and when I got back to the bar I put the key back where I had found it. Sentimental. I knew no-one was coming back for that key. Whatever had happened in this town was now over.

I left Weston the way I had first come; by the overland route to the motorway. And feeling as lost. There were no police-stops or road-blocks, and not a single car was in sight as I joined the slow-lane and began pushing south.

I felt nothing except pain. Something about the forlorn

little pile of clothes beside me on the front seat was screaming more tunelessly than ever that Johanna was dead. It was the final joker of a revelation. A pile of obscene underwear.

I hardly even noticed when the radio started headlining news of the arrest.

Chapter Four

Over the mainland of Europe, a prolonged snowstorm had made the Berlin air-corridor into a sickening switchback.

A desert of snow, interspersed by a few trough-like roads, spread out below the bumping and diving plane. When we finally nosed our way down onto the ice-grey tarmac of Tegel Airport I felt a surge of relief. Partly because the flight was over but more just to be out of England.

During the month since my interview with Paines I had almost begun to wish I was back on the run. There was no further evidence and the 'murderer' awaited trial. The brown spots on Marie's five pound note had been analysed as mud and, since she had been reported missing by her parents for months, her continued disappearance meant very little. Worse, John was forced to publish a retraction of his story after Paines had hinted to his paper's editor that the allegations of CURV corruption were sufficient grounds for a libel action. From a crusading fugitive I was reduced to an impotent crank. Even John tried to discourage me from further investigation.

Back in my flat I took to sleeping late and eating badly. One morning I was looking blankly through the accumulation of unopened mail when I saw a cryptic post-card with a photo of a frozen lake surrounded by snow. 'This is how you imagine it,' it said, 'but you're wrong.' It took me too long to realise it was from Karen. I tried to write her a lengthy explanatory letter but hardly one page left my typewriter. Then after a few weeks I dipped into my savings and flew to Berlin. I had managed to trace Werner Kullen.

Paines had described him as a social theorist and, once I had deduced that it was spelled with a K, the name was unusual enough to make it easy. A study he had done on urbanisation and the Navajo in parts of Arizona had quite a circulation. From what I could gather the man was half-

124

German and half-American, but at one time he had held a lecturing job in Birmingham.

A visit to the Department of Anthropology at Birmingham University revealed Kullen had left three years earlier. The secretary turned out to be a bouncy twinset and pearls who obviously enjoyed any opportunity to gossip. She lost no time at all in fishing out his forwarding address in Berlin.

'Some glamorous thesis for UNESCO or something, lucky stiff,' she said, squinting at the card. 'They pay a fortune so he'd better organise it better than his one here.'

'What happened to that?' I said as I wrote down the address.

'Another unfinished masterpiece,' she said slotting the card back into the file. 'He came here to do some study on the ghastly old new towns. No that sounds wrong; can a new town be old?'

'Like Cumbernauld, Weston, Corby etcetera?' I said helpfully.

'Umm, that sort of thing. But he left bang in the middle of it. I wasn't around then but I think his marriage broke up or something. Anyway there was nothing to show for a couple of years work and the Prof was livid. Apparently said he's never employ another American. *That* didn't last long.'

The same day I wrote, requesting a research interview for my book, to the address in West Berlin, which was a hotel, but heard nothing. A phone call established that it was simply a forwarding address, and by now I was so curious about Werner Kullen that I decided to waste no more time.

He turned out to be living at 26 Rungestrasse which was fine in theory until I realised it was in East Berlin.

Crossing the wall is no longer an ordeal for a tourist but only those with an iron sense of personal security could actually enjoy it. Since few taxis were venturing out in the thick snow I had a dreary walk from my hotel to Friedrichstrasse, where the gunmetal grey uniforms of the guards seemed particularly unwelcoming.

There are four layers of communist protocol at Checkpoint Charlie and today, perhaps because of the intense cold, each one was more bloody-minded than the last. To make matters worse, I had stupidly forgotten to remove from my case a spy paperback showing a hammer and sickle prominently displayed alongside a jackboot. The blonde red-cheeked guard going through the case was so enraged that for a moment I thought he was going to hit me across the face. He screamed abuse in incomprehensible German until his superior, a small dark-haired man, came through to see what was the matter. He simply tore the book up in my face and waved me on.

I think I had expected Kullen to be living in one of the huge tower-blocks that dominate East Berlin like sacred shrines. As with everything else in this miracle of reconstruction, these towers cater for every imaginable kind of human need – except the most basic need of all for a human scale. To drive through the Communist part of the city is a revelation, to walk through it is a nightmare.

Fortunately Rungestrasse was within two miles of the Checkpoint and I wandered in between the looming skyscrapers, intrigued to see graffiti on the Communist walls and an endless series of potted plants in the windows. I crossed a bridge over one of the dank smelly tributaries of the Spree and plunged into a pretty school square where two bears were playing in a spacious cage.

Then I began to find myself back in pre-war Berlin. Old twisted streets, obviously due for demolition but still very much inhabited, loomed up on either side, five storey buildings of crumbling beauty with ancient wooden doors giving onto huge dark hallways and everywhere the smell of soup. None of these back streets had been cleared of snow and a few cars lay shored up in the drifts like marooned battleships.

Apart from my feet crunching in the snow, the only sound was the crackle of icicles above, giving way to their own weight. Rungestrasse was sandwiched right in the middle of the maze, the most dilapidated street of all, a bizarre cul-de-sac which ended abruptly in a fenced industrial wasteland behind a black sign reading VEB ENERGIE KOMBINAT.

The windows on the street were dark and the doorways huge and closed. 26 was the last house on the block. The perfect refuge. Like something out of an East European fairy-tale.

The front door opened with difficulty onto a hall that hadn't been cleaned since the war. Dust and plaster covered the walls. Under the filth the remains of elegant stucco tiles had been left to disintegrate.

On the ground floor doorway was a faded sign: 'Hans

Ritter, Buchbinderei.' I walked up the ancient stone staircase. The bell on the first landing didn't work so I rapped on the heavy old door and found it was open.

The room was so dark that I had to screw up my eyes to make anything out. There was not much furniture but it was big and warm and dusty. In the dim light I could see numerous little piles of books and a long line of bottles running along the floor. Lingering on the threshold, I knocked against one and it clattered loudly against the wall.

I jumped when I saw the shape; it was sprawled in a far corner under a small reading light. Two round lenses glinted in my direction. Otherwise all I could make out was a thick old rug twisted and bulging. Suddenly it began to move, and grunted at me.

'Come on, come on,' it waved me impatiently towards it. 'And, Jesus Christ, shut the door! It's cold enough to come crushed ice out there.'

I stood there uncertainly. 'Yeah, I knew you were coming,' it said exasperatedly, still beckoning me over to the fire. You can ring East-West now and the hotel calls if anyone comes looking for me. Now sit down and have a drink for Chrissakes.'

Kullen sat up in his seat with a glass in his hand and his bright eyes surveyed me as I grew accustomed to the grey afternoon light seeping through the dirty windows. He was in his fifties with sparse grey hair. The thick glasses and Germanic exuberance made him look a little like a caricature psychiatrist, but there was something slightly cruder about him. The New York part. His clothes were crumpled and dirty and the occasional sparks of German in his speech were drowned by Manhattan.

He waved my letter under my nose. 'Too much else to do to reply,' he said, 'but now you're here you can suck off me all you like for your book. What do you want to know?'

He took a swig from his glass and began refilling an old pipe. 'How's the UNESCO work?' I said as I picked a pile of books and papers from the other chair and sat down. There was nothing inappropriate about the books in the room. They were exactly what you would expect from someone mugging up on socially and politically divided communities: Belfast, Jerusalem, South Africa.

'Oh fine,' he replied, pulling unsuccessfully on his pipe.

'They pay me a lot of marks to talk to people affected by the wall in one way or another. It's a big worthy mound of bullshit and it keeps me happy.'

He saw me staring surreptitiously at the state of the apartment. 'Yeah, I know. You're wondering what happens to all those UNESCO marks. Well, they aren't under the rug. A lot of them go back to my ex-wife who has extravagant New York tastes. On top of that a man has to pay to fuck and that comes expensive around here.' He watched me with amusement, hoping for a reaction. 'But if you want to know the truth,' he sat back in his chair, 'the mindfucking truth is that this is the prettiest street in this whole city, if not in the whole country. And believe it or not I actually *want* to live here like this in a heap of shit and not in some air-conditioned fuckpad.'

'No visa problem?' I asked.

'Hell, no,' he said, lifting his glasses and rubbing his eyes. 'The Eastern boys love this thesis. It's one of those humanitarian heaps of bullshit they wrote into the last SALT. I'm just the bastard who does it.'

Now he sat there, waiting for me to start asking him questions. I had glanced at some of Kullen's work on the Navajo and launched straight into it. His answers were impressive but he was still rather suspicious. Pretty soon I knew I wouldn't find any cracks in his crude mental armour so I played the only hand I had. I told him I wasn't there to talk about my book. I was there to talk about Paines.

It was as though I'd dangled a piece of dead flesh in front of his face. For the first time he really reacted. Then he got up and glared out of the window and asked if I'd come alone.

Eventually he seemed to believe me. You could hardly find a more difficult street in which to conceal someone.

'You know,' said Kullen turning ruefully back from the window, 'the Chicanos say that if you let it hang out too far the man will cut it off. This is the risk you now have to take, my friend.'

I told him what had happened to me. At first he kept staring out the window. Then he sat back down forgetting about his glass and concentrating directly on the bottle. 'Oh Christ!' he muttered every few minutes. When I mentioned about the prostitutes and the murders, he glared at me as though it was an irrelevance. 'Doesn't fit,' he muttered. 'Crazy.'

After I had finished there was a long pause.

'OK, two items,' he said at last. 'One: I lied to you a few minutes ago. This is a pretty street but I'm not here because it's pretty. I'm here because it helps me sleep. I can vet anyone who ever wants to see me like I did with you. And the big bad wall is wonderful security. Two: what I know I cannot prove and it would only get me killed if I could. So don't start screaming "Onward Christian Soldiers" at me after you've heard it. I'm not interested.'

I nodded. Kullen emptied his bottle and opened another. He didn't seem drunk but I noticed the flow of obscenities was drying up. I was only slowly beginning to realise they were a rather ragged cover for fear.

'Hell,' he said, 'I've been doing my damnedest to forget. And why not? No reason on God's earth why I should remember it. Every country's screwed up, not just yours and mine. . . .' He trailed off, wiping his mouth on his sleeve, his thick eyebrows wrinkling in concentration.

'It began because I was doing some very ordinary background research on your new towns. Standard bullshit thesis stuff. Not even a particularly original subject. But I began to get very interested in the overall history of the period. The fifties. I was going into it in a lot of detail. A hell of a lot of detail.'

'You see, after studying the Navajo it interested me how women are always dragged into the labour force for a war. And then after the war they're pitched back into the nursery. The consequence of this in a sophisticated western society, like Britain in the fifties, is that you get a prize heap of media obsessions. For ten years, the Royal Family is on the cover of every newspaper, especially their children. You have an awful lot of crap about families. And you even have the most important psychologists in the land like Bowlby screaming about maternal deprivation and saying mummy love is the same as vitamins and proteins. All kinds of social forces with a mutual interest.'

The change in Kullen was spectacular. Despite his half-crazed appearance, as he got into his subject, he could have been lecturing a group of students.

'Now I am going through all this stuff,' he took a pull at

129

his bottle, 'and I find that in 1953 one of the most patriotic British newspapers, the Express, actually runs a 'Rebuild Britain' contest. The title 'Mothering Village of the Year' is going to be offered to the little village with the highest percentage of births in the twelve months ending Mother's Day 1953. So what? It was just one of these little foot-notes. Then I notice that our old friend Weston is one of the villages making a big play for the title. Claiming a record number of births. This was way before the new development there of course. It was still just a tiny village. That interests me a little. But what interests me a damn sight more is that its figures get disqualified.'

He pulled at his grey hair. 'Yeah, I suppose you could say that was when the whole fucking mess began. Jesus Christ, I think, was someone fixing the hospital returns or were they giving birth to mutants or what? So I get out a pile of microfilm. And I could see why the Express got pissed off.' He paused: 'The old village had a high incidence of inbreeding. It just would not have looked too good as 'England's Mothering Village'! There were plenty of interesting court-cases around that time: incest, parental cruelty. The place was a rural slum.'

He took another long pull at his bottle. 'Nothing too unusual about that. Small isolated population, backward way of life. Plenty of other villages in England like that in the 50s. But Weston interested me because unlike the others it had a new industrial site on its hands and the planners soon had their eye on it. They opened the first part of the new estate in the sixties. Not that big a scheme. About a thousand families at first. It was overshadowed in the media by much more impressive developments in the south. But there was something special about this moonscape. In its sweet little way it was a twenty-four carat classic. Even for then. And that my friend is saying something.'

He got up throwing the last words over his shoulder at me and went to check the street. It was getting darker in the room but he didn't put the light on.

'So bearing that in mind,' he sat back down, 'I went right on studying these microfilms. And you know the cuttings get worse not better.'

'I can still see them,' he said closing his eyes. 'A twelve-year-old girl's father is arrested when his daughter dies in a home abortion attempt. A few months later another honey: a man was accused of raping his daughter by a family cousin but the parents deny the charge and he gets off. Then a father is deprived of the custody of his two daughters after allegations of sexual impropriety. Some of these cases made the nationals, plenty more didn't. The social workers found it heavy going. One of them wrote a bitter article about the new town's problems.

'It was a planner's nightmare. The real article. All of the studies since the war have shown the same degree of introversion in slum families badly rehoused. But good old fucking Weston had gone one better. Somehow they had managed to get the two prize recipes for social withdrawal into the same bed. Urban alienation and rural isolation: feeding off each other. Like I said it was a masterpiece. Someone deserved a medal.' He took another drink.

'But this was still early days. People were getting wise about planning. And there was much more public awareness that all was not exactly sunshine mellow with some of the new schemes. There was even, God help us, a bit of quiet horror here and there, especially when the energy crisis increased the isolation factor as the price of petrol rose. But then some curious rays of light begin to appear in the town. Less vandalism, maybe even a little less street crime. People are staying inside at night and making their children do the same. Juvenile delinquency, which had been quite serious in the early days of the estate, starts to decline. Also the engineering works and the other heavy industries begin to have a staggeringly good industrial record. This is all trumpeted in the local press and, when you think about it, it figures. You see sexual and social introversion on that kind of scale breeds passivity and an increase in paternal authority. A bit like reintroducing a sharp and concentrated dose of the Victorian era. When you look at the chaos that was happening in the rest of England at this time, the street battles and the industrial disputes, is it any wonder people began to take an interest?

'For a while the family cases keep on coming. Battered children, incest, gross parental neglect. Until quite suddenly they stop. Just like that. There isn't another one. And from under the blanket our crime-free model community begins to emerge.

'And that, my friend, is when I really started to get worried as hell. Social phenomena never stop dead. None of the other crime figures had. The best they can do for us fallible humans is pan out on a graph and die away. But this graph was a cliff-face and it ended *exactly around* the time of the curfews. It smacked of deliberate, calculated human intervention. Someone had simply taken the decision to let the families go their own way. Who cared whether the shit was in the home as long as it wasn't cluttering up the street? Weston wasn't a town anymore. It was a damned laboratory. The incest-as-fun show.'

I struggled to keep up with him. 'OK, so they stopped prosecuting people for messing around with their children. . . .'

'Oh come on,' he shouted at me. 'You know damn well if you know anything, that about the main thing anthropology has turned up this century is the fact that the prohibition of certain close relatives as sexual partners is completely basic, a stone core of human behaviour. Things like money or food are insignificant beside it. OK, we still don't properly understand its function but we do know that incest sure as hell isn't just an interesting kink like flagellation. Its taboo is basic to the way we live, the way we organise, the way we think. And dabbling in it on a large scale, if it were possible, would probably be more dangerous than fiddling with human genes or cloned babies. A modern Frankenstein would be into kinship reorganization, not bits of corpses.'

'Surely you aren't saying,' I objected 'that from the 60s a majority of the population of Weston were committing incest. That seems unlikely even on a desert island.'

'No,' said Kullen, slapping his frayed trouser leg with his palm. 'I'm saying that due to an extraordinary combination of factors a *significant minority* began to turn inwards, socially retreating into family groups. Others would be living normally, because in a town of sufficient size there is nothing to stop the two things existing side by side.

'But you must know that once you get withdrawal on that kind of scale in an isolated geographical situation it becomes a creeping growth. I've seen it elsewhere. Straight families will find the atmosphere bad, their neighbours hostile, their neighbours' children introverted and precocious. But they won't know why. Because incest isn't something conducted

132

in public. So gradually the normals are going to retreat into their own shells or move elsewhere. And if they don't, their kids certainly will.'

His voice dropped away. 'What we're finally talking about here is the death of the community in the most literal sense of the term. Because an incestuous community, even a partially incestuous community, isn't really a community at all. It's a number of tiny disconnected closed systems, a social atomization zone. We've all experienced this in degrees before, the idea that a town is dying, that people aren't going out to each other. Weston was just taken a little further and pushed over the edge.'

'The subversion of a whole community?' I said it with a mixture of disbelief and wonder.

'Not quite,' said Kullen. 'Just the maintenance of a strange and fruitful cultural mutation. That was the way it was put to me.' He pulled a face, 'Right now it's a rather fine distinction.'

The level of anxiety was rising in the room with the darkness. Almost as if he was taking a reading, Kullen got up to make another inspection from the window. I realised as he returned to his chair that his manner earlier had been an attempt to deceive me. He might once have been the absent-minded professor with a comical line in obscenities but there was nothing vague about the fear I saw now.

'I was damn stupid,' he said eventually. 'Because I rang up the police and started asking questions. A few days later Paines came to see me at the university. He talked about the marvellous crime figures in the town and about being a bit liberal for the greater good of the community. Put his case well and asked me not to publish. We row and he leaves. Two nights later, my wife is run over. They never trace the killer.'

He looked away. 'Yes, I lied to you. She's dead. You see we weren't even happy. The divorce was going through. But Paines killed her anyway. Phut!'

There were tears in his eyes. Now he'd finished, he seemed to shrink into his chair and I sensed his terrible guilt. Kullen would never finish his UNESCO thesis. He would cower here as long as he possibly could and then he would die of something stupid, probably influenza brought on by drink and neglect.

'The people I talked to thought I was mad,' he said in reply to my silent accusations. 'Especially about the incest. They thought her death had pushed me over.'

'But why didn't you publish anyway? If they can't get you here?'

Kullen laughed hysterically. There was something collapsed about him. The obscenities now came out shrill and feeble.

'That's the mindfucking pathos of this whole shitty mess. Don't you see that by any scientific standards I *have* nothing to publish. Just a few freak statistics and a mass of assumption. No serious periodical would touch it anymore than they'd eat my crap off the sidewalk. How *can* you have hard scientific evidence for what people are doing privately in their own homes? What are we supposed to do? A house-to-house survey. The only reason Paines feared me was because he thought anthropology was some wizard Sherlock Holmes subject that can pin down communities like butterflies. The real joke is he never had to worry.'

'So what do you think will happen in the town?' I asked after a while. I wanted to get out of the flat more than anything. I dreaded Kullen would ask me to stay and hold his hand. 'What will happen in a few years?'

'I don't know,' Kullen said. 'Because of the murders they've probably returned the whole thing to square one. The operation will be closed down. But anyway it isn't going to work like they hoped. No passive ordered society. No chance.'

'Well, what might happen?' I pushed.

'You can't make a prediction,' he said. 'There's nothing to go on. Not in the past. Not in anthropology.'

Then something seemed to occur to him: 'Of course Freud did have a theory about a society along those lines once. In one of his early works.'

'And that was?'

His laughter was hollow.

'The children eat the fathers,' he said.

PART 4

CLIMAX

'Incestuous relationships only appear contradictory to family sentiments because we have conceived of the latter as irreducibly excluding the former. . . . But if a long and ancient tradition allowed men to marry their near relatives . . . sexual life would not have become what it is . . . It would have a less personal character, and would have less room for the free play of the imagination, dreams and the spontaneities of desire.'

Claude Levi-Strauss: *The Elementary Structures of Kinship*

Chapter One

Hotel lobbies are never the homeliest of places, but there can be few in the world as daunting as the hallway of the Contemporary Resort Hotel in Lake Buena Vista, Florida. At least the size of a football-field in length and nine stories high, it is dominated by a garish floor-to-roof mural of no less than 18000 hand-painted ceramic tiles. Above you a monorail noses its way through the fourth floor like a rapacious snake, and camera-snapping tourists stare down.

That expression of rapt expectation had become familiar to me over the last few days, because the Contemporary is a part of Walt Disney World's famed tourist complex. Its smart shops and restaurants are designed as some kind of haven from the noisy crowds. And in all that space, the hotel staff can observe you for miles as you pad over the green carpet through the potted trees towards them. It is not an easy place to be inconspicuous.

That's why I sat as unobtrusively as possible in one of the oases of armchairs as Andrew Paines stepped out of the lift. I had been watching him and his elegant wife on and off for three days. Most of the time it had been impossible to follow them consistently without taking the risk of being seen; twice I had sat buried in a book as they dined enthusiastically at the Top of the World supper club; the previous afternoon I had watched from my own room as they took the boat-trip to Discovery Island and returned looking cold and bored. Once I very nearly stumbled into them head-on outside the Sand Bar. I was only saved by a weather-beaten old man in a tracksuit who chose that moment to accost them about England's troubles.

The English press had dutifully recorded Paines's fact-finding holiday to study Walt Disney World's globally acclaimed security system. After a futile attempt to confirm what Kullen had said in Berlin, I knew Paines was the only person in the

137

world who could tell me what I wanted to know about Johanna.

Clutching the small case I had kept beside me since London and keeping a good distance, I watched him enter one of the bars. It was nine o'clock at night and this was the first time I had seen him without his wife. I hesitated because I wanted to see what he would do. Eventually he headed up towards the monorail platform.

The monorail is the most direct link between the Contemporary Hotel and the resort's famous amusement park: the Magic Kingdom. At one time this had been Walt Disney World's number one attraction but much of its glory had recently been stolen by the opening of Walt's pet dream, the long-planned EPCOT centre, the 'Experimental Community of Tomorrow', with its totally futuristic environment. I knew Paines had already visited EPCOT twice and now, as he was brandishing a half-used book of Magic Kingdom tickets, I guessed it was the end of his trip and he was making a brief solo excursion to use up the last of their passes.

As the monorail doors slid open I stepped in behind him and took a seat adjacent to his, keeping the bag on my knee. The train ran smoothly out of the hotel into the darkness. I could see a little shock go through Paines as he recognised me, but he recovered well.

'Holiday?' he said, shifting in his seat with a polite puzzled smile, obviously hoping this was just an unhappy coincidence.

I shook my head. 'No, I've seen it before.'

His expression became momentarily grimmer. Then he smiled. 'Ah.' A pause. 'You'd have been better to waylay me on some English country lane.'

He wasn't joking. Disney World's security had always been legendary but in recent years it had effectively prevented urban violence from penetrating Disney's empire at all. The park was guarded via TV and computer from the miles of service area directly beneath it: the occasional purse-snatch was usually isolated with devastating speed.

The guide tape clicked on and began extolling the wonders of the Magic Kingdom. The train was approaching the monorail station.

'I want you to tell me about Johanna,' I said. He shrugged: 'The killer has been arrested. He should be convicted.'

A bubble-gum chewing child squinted at us from the other

side of the aisle as the train stopped. We filed out of the station towards the Magic Kingdom's main entrance, and the blaze of lights beyond.

A thin drizzle had begun to fall. It had been a colder winter than usual in Florida and, with the rival attraction of EP-COT, the park seemed strangely desolate. Little groups of ghost-like families moved through the turnstile. Inside, people looked strained by fatigue and the weather. Paines seemed to become more animated as he saw how empty it was. 'Minorities night,' he murmured.

We walked up the sloping pavement and emerged on Main Street, USA, the slightly scaled-down replica of an old Western street. Eerily illuminated in the distance against the night sky were the soaring blue spires of Cinderella's castle. A boy with Mickey Mouse ears ran by shouting angrily after his mother. A multitude of coloured lights were picked up crazily by the thin stream of rain. I had been here before in pleasanter circumstances but tonight it looked nightmarish.

Paines turned to me confidingly, pointing at the smooth asphalt at our feet. 'There are several hundred people down there,' he said. 'They work while we play.'

I didn't reply. I was waiting without much hope to see if the sheer unlikeliness of the meeting might lower his guard in some way.

Like its near-duplicate in Disneyland California, Florida's Magic Kingdom is based on a hub system with four distinctive 'lands' of amusement radiating out from a circle of which Cinderella's castle is the centre. It is designed on the assumption that the crowd will tend to move anti-clockwise. Paines was determined to behave as if I wasn't there and now cut right across the traffic towards the extremity of Adventureland, in the lefthand corner of the park. As we weaved our way through the exhausted crowds heading back to Main Street, I was jostled by an angry couple arguing about whose turn it was to carry a kid that had gone to sleep. There were loud rifle reports from the Frontierland shooting gallery.

'I saw Kullen in Berlin,' I said through the melee.

He kept walking, his eyes straight ahead. To our right, people were streaming out of the Enchanted Tiki Birds. We seemed to be heading for the 'Pirates of the Caribbean', one of Disney's oldest and most famous rides.

'I know what happened in the town,' I shouted against the noise of audio displays and yelling kids.

'Yes?' said Paines neutrally as he grinned at a little girl in a mohair cowboy suit.

'Its sexual behaviour seems to have fallen a little out of line with the image.'

'For instance?' said Paines. We took our place in the queue for the Pirates ride.

'Do you call incest sane and healthy?'

'No,' he said, still without looking at me. 'But how do you expect us to supervise what people are up to in their own homes? I'm only a policeman.' His favourite line.

'You let it happen.'

He shrugged: 'You can only judge social behaviour by its effects. If people want to reorganise their sex life, that's a pretty small price to pay for a crime-free community.'

'Yes,' I said. 'Living corpses make model citizens.'

We were getting closer to the 'Pirates' turnstile and Paines turned to me with his most amused look. But now I could catch some of the hatred beneath it.

'You are a romantic,' he said softly. 'Out of time and out of place. You want people to behave like savages in public just to prove life's rich diversity. Weston has been left alone now. But we can do the same thing somewhere else. And the reason why is that people want us to. They *want* us to clean the streets. Why don't you ask them?'

I thought of the Law-and-Order Referendum in England. A couple of years earlier it had come down massively in favour of tougher laws against crime.

The queue turned a corner and we could see the sparkling lagoon from which the bright long boats dropped out of sight to the automated labyrinth below. The children in front of us were laughing and screaming in anticipation.

'You didn't ask the children,' I said.

He shrugged again: 'Does any system? They were protected by the people who cared for them most.'

His voice merged with the splash from the head of the line as each boat tumbled down into the grotto. There were shrieks of delight from the disappearing riders, and a buzz of excitement from behind us.

The sheer coolness of his reasoning was infuriating. We might have been discussing legal theory.

'They were the victims,' I shouted. People looked round but Paines ignored me. It was soon our turn to take seats at the side of one of the longboats. I still clutched my blue zipper bag.

The craft jerked forward and after a couple of bends we plunged gravityless into the darkness.

The main portion of Pirates of the Caribbean is a smooth water journey through vast illuminated caverns, populated by frantic automated pirates in various scenarios. Although the robots can't actually walk, the combination of lip, eye and limb movement together with their incessant pirate chatter gives an uncanny illusion of life.

Paines stared at the procession of scenes before us but I could tell he was coiled like a spring.

The other riders had their eyes fixed on the action as I played my last card. Slowly unzipping the bag on my knee, I brought out a fistful of the garish hooker underwear I'd found in Weston: satin crotchless pants, open nipple bra. In that setting, suffused in reds and yellows by the trick flashes from a pirate cannon it looked more tawdry and bizarre than ever.

And for the first time Paines reacted: his eyes shone with anger as I held the stuff deliberately close to his face.

'From that deserted pub in Weston,' I said. 'Your men must have missed it. In a place where sex is being shoved back into the closet, why an outbreak of old-fashioned porno?'

Some people were looking round at us now. A bespectacled man with a young daughter squinted angrily at what was in my hand, then turned away. There was no mistaking the intensity of Paines's expression but he pretended to be distracted by a prison scene of a pirate trying to get cell keys from a little robot dog with a wagging tail.

'That was not a natural development,' he said eventually. 'The two women involved were romantics like you. They weren't in it for money.'

'Then what were they doing?' Our conversation was once again being drowned by the noise.

'They were trying to break up the town's social pattern,' he said. 'But they didn't understand what was involved.'

'You mean they knew the town was dying but they didn't know a government agency was sticking the knife in.'

'They didn't know the harm they were doing,' Paines said.

141

'So you stopped them.'

Just that. It was so simple I cursed my failure to see it. Now I understood why the salesman's fantasy-filled account of Johanna had always made a certain kind of sense. Because it *was* a fantasy. The two girls, Jo and Jane, hadn't been real prostitutes at all; their purpose wasn't economic. Somehow they had stumbled across what was happening in Weston and systematically and aggressively they had tried to attack the monster's jugular. By recreating sexual fantasy in the town, the one thing its stifling enclosed atmosphere could never absorb. Even the worst and crudest kind of male fantasy was better than no fantasy at all.

We were reaching the most spectacular part of the ride where a legion of pirates on all sides of the boat engage in a fierce and noisy conflict. The clash of steel and cannon-fire matched my moment of revelation. 'So someone hit on an idea that solved all your problems at one stroke,' I said. 'That allows you to bring in more men and equipment, that gets rid of the girls *and* sends the inhabitants scurrying back to their sex holes.'

Paines turned back to me, his face a weird assortment of colours from the blaze around us but every inch telling me that I was right. 'And what was this idea?'

'The killings,' I said. 'The town was a closed system. Nobody was going to suspect political motives behind a sex murder. It was the perfect way of cementing the status quo.'

The children in the boat shrieked as a pirate chief told them to prepare for squalls ahead. But the waterfall that followed was the ride's last gimmick and we were back in the entrance-hall.

Paines said, 'I don't see that I have to listen to your drivel any longer.' And he pushed his way out of the boat.

By the time I emerged from the exit he was moving quickly towards Liberty Square and Frontierland. I suppose I should have been more suspicious. If he wanted to get rid of me all he had to do was call a security guard. But I was desperate to know the last piece of the jigsaw, the piece about Johanna, and all I could think about was not letting him get away.

Pushing through a knot of gum-chewing children I saw him melt into the crowd by the Frontierland shooting gallery. It was raining harder now and the swept asphalt below me was slippery. Shouting his name I pushed past the gallery into Liberty Square, nearly knocking over an old lady coming out of one of the tourist shops. I wondered if the chase was already being monitored on TV screens below us.

Some of the crowd had now taken refuge from the rain in the Hall of Presidents and the Liberty Tavern so it wasn't hard to spot him moving rapidly out of the far end of the square. We were near the top end of the park and he was gaining distance.

I ran faster, slipping madly around the obstructions and nearly stunning myself against one of the fancy Fantasyland lamp-posts. I was already soaked and when I stumbled and fell on the concrete at the top of the park I thought I had lost him.

Then I saw his thin blue figure walking up the steps to the Skyway cable-car which serves as a means of transport from one side of the park to the other.

Families were crowding onto the Skyway to avoid getting wet but I was able to get on a few cars behind Paines.

Below me, pinpointed on the clear waters of the Jules Verne lagoon as I swung across the park, was Disney's menacing fleet of Nautilus submarines from *Twenty Thousand Leagues Under the Sea*. Their fish-eyed portholes glared venemously up, reminding me of how much I dreaded the controlled environment in which this game was being played. Especially since Paines was far more familiar with it than I was.

The cable-car executed a neat corner and the vast white planetarium structure of the Space Mountain loomed up in front of us.

We docked at the Tomorrowland Terminal, not far from the castle and the main entrance. But Paines did not head in that direction. Instead he hurried through the entrance of the Space Mountain itself.

Half of me didn't want to follow. I had no reason to think he would tell me anything else. But the tantalizing illumination he'd already provided was too much. I ran up the ramp of the dark winding catwalk which leads up to the indoor roller coaster.

Chapter Two

The Space Mountain had once been Disney World's most popular ride but, in spite of some recent renovation, it was now comparatively empty. There were no queues looking at the videotapes of the ride's twisting highlights as I reached the top of the gantry. Only a few expectant riders clustered around the loading platforms for the two tracks on each side of the stairs. Obsessively I searched their faces but Paines was not among them. I began to think he had already taken the ride down.

I stood there alone for a few moments and eventually took a seat in the front of one of the two-seater tubular cars on the Alpha track. A friendly Disney guide joked about my dishevelled appearance as she checked the safety-bar was secure, so I failed to notice the other rider slipping into the slot behind.

The car jerked its way into a round launching shaft, where expectation was deliberately intensified by a deafening klaxon and pulsating lines of red light.

The 'Prepare to Launch' sign had flashed and we were sliding forward when I became conscious of the thin sharp point under my left shoulder-blade. Rather like the touch of an animal's claw.

Wrenching around in my seat I could see an amused face in the flickering red light. Paines smiled from the seat behind mine and there was something in his hand.

'Of course we killed Johanna,' he said. And pushed the knife slowly into my back.

It was too late to get out. No matter how far forward against the safety-bar I squeezed, the pressure followed. And Paines had evidently baited his trap with care. He would know the ride and its control-room: there are limits to what infra-red cameras can see and even greater limits to the patience of those who monitor them.

A wet numbness began to creep down my spine as the car catapaulted its way along the invisible track into a series of fast banked turns. At any point Paines could have lunged but he preferred toying with me, pinioned against my safety-bar, wielding the long thin knife with surgical precision. As the pain sharpened in the blackness, I sensed the pleasure behind it.

There was no chance of being seen by another rider. Pitch darkness is the Space Mountain's chief asset over other rollercoasters. This deliberately increases its savage sense of momentum so that at every moment the ride seems about to hurtle off the track.

When he twisted the knife in I screamed. But the noise simply reverberated around the black arena with all the other screams and yells.

Now the car went into a jolting climb and the force sent me back against the blade so hard that everything disappeared into the hole opening up in my back.

I was snatched out of unconsciousness by a dazzling burst of electronic meteorites. These herald the Space Mountain's biggest free-fall drop, and Paines must have been sufficiently worried by the sudden illumination to relax his pressure.

I sensed it and at that moment of near-motionlessness before the apex of the ride, I fumbled round behind me to try and grab the blade with my hand. The clarity of the pain as it cut a shallow gash in my palm goaded me on. The knife raked across my shoulder in a furrow of agony that made me cry out again, but I clamped his wrist with my hand before he could redirect it and twisted myself under the safety-bar to throw myself back towards his face. Before the car could dive into free-fall, I had crawled on top of him, and locked my arms round his neck.

The whole world spun away from me as I clung on. His head and shoulders were taking most of the weight of my body, my nails digging deep into his neck.

His head was pushed right forward and I felt him writhe in pain, as the rest of me dangled sickeningly from the car.

He tried to bring the blade back and would have killed me with it but the force of my weight was hauling him out of the car. The knife slashed ineffectually at thin air.

As we hit the bottom of the dip I dragged my legs into the car on top of him. He must have known the high-speed corner

145

that followed the drop because, just as we went into it, his mouth found my wrist and bit down viciously as he brought his knee hard into my groin.

The spasm of pain forced me off him gasping on my side, clinging to the safety-bar. And in the dim orange light I caught a glimpse of his face glistening with sweat and triumph as he forced himself out and under the bar to bring the blade plunging into my stomach. There was no way I could stop him.

People are not supposed to give way to messy reflexes in death-struggle but they do. As Paines was about to rip me wide open, I should have risen to some life-saving feat. But instead I started vomiting. The stomach-churning momentum and the terror gave way to a helpless retching and Paines paused.

It was pure contempt. I must have looked like a pathetic specimen to kill.

Then the knife came down. But in that moment of revulsion he had forgotten the Space Mountain's addiction to surprises. A fast and unexpected half-way hump is designed to take your breath away and because of his artistic delay we hit it just as he was putting all his energy into the final execution. His blow was knocked sideways. The knife missed my chest and the force of the swing sent him flailing into mid-air. For a moment he was suspended, half-in and half-out of the car, one leg dangling in space as the knife spun away into the darkness. Then he went over the side.

It was a long time before the impact but there was only the fast whine of the car on the metal tracks. I wish he had screamed.

The kids at the bottom were at the close of a long and boring shift and they didn't notice the bloody hole in the back of my jacket. I cleaned up as best as I could in one of the toilets and took the monorail straight to the car park.

I drove for some time but as it turned out I need not have worried about the death catching up with me. Disney have their own ambulance system and there is nothing the company likes less than major news stories about casualties inside their parks. It was not until months later that the English press unearthed some of the more picturesque facts surrounding Paines's 'accident'. No-one made any sense of the knife but sometimes I wondered about how they reacted to the blue zipper bag that would have turned up in the bottom of one of the pirate boats.

Somehow, like everything else, that little bundle of dream-stuff seemed fated to oblivion. I knew one thing: in a million years Disney would never publicise its contents.

PART 5

WITHDRAWAL

'Louise she's all right, she's just near.'

Bob Dylan: *Visions of Johanna*

Chapter One

In the late twentieth century, solutions are like political parties. You need a strong injection of money or influence before they get believed. Even then they have to be diluted and easy to understand. Mine was neither.

Back in London John helped me to try and find proof. If Johanna was killed in order to protect the anti-crime experiment in Weston, then the death of Weatherspoon, the MP, was part of the same cover-up. But our last attempt to put the story into print had been an ignominious failure and even now we had little that was more concrete except my conversation with Paines, which was unusable if I wanted to avoid becoming a murder suspect.

Everything in Weston had appeared to return to normal. There was even a much-publicised incest case which generated considerable local scandal; a well-meaning editorial appeared in the local press about getting the town's social problems right once and for all.

Privately I believed the experiment had been thrown into reverse and wondered if this last shift might not have an even worse effect than anything else. Like adding a violent new element to an already unstable atomic pile. Yet the town continued quiet and anonymous.

I moved back into my old flat and for the rest of that summer, with the money I had left, I made tentative fruitless investigations. But most of my crusading spirit had evaporated. After Paines's death, it was like trying to ransack a room from which everything had been removed. The other conspirators were faceless shadows. And now that, in spite of my past suspicions, I knew Johanna was the thing in the morgue some of my questing instincts had died with her.

It was mainly out of a sense of duty that I tried to set up a meeting with the defence lawyer in Johanna's murder trial. Then the news came that the accused man, Wright, had made a dash from a police car outside Hull on a mercy visit to his sick mother, and got clean away. There were reliable civilian witnesses to the escape and later it was given out that he may have been harboured by friends and seen out of the country.

As far as I was concerned it was transparent. Much better for them than a trial.

Now the whole thing was in a perfect state of suspension. No victim, no murderer, no prosecution. The papers swallowed it whole, there were scandalised arguments about security and the granting of requests by prisoners' relatives. My subsequent interview with Wright's lawyer was distinctly unsuccessful; he obviously regarded me as a crank.

Around that time I used to dream of just one break. Like a policeman coming forward and saying he'd lied. It was just a dream.

By the autumn, as nothing else materialised and the money ran low, I was forced back to a few magazine assignments, which I did badly, trading on old loyalties. A freezing east wind had begun an early assault on London, emptying the streets and parks. In my obsessive activity I had barely noticed the summer at all, and now I was confronted with another plunge into dark and cold. Back in my flat, I stayed in bed late, eating little. My life became almost mechanical. The few letters I opened contained cheques. I noticed two or three airletters from Finland but I never read them.

One freezing morning Karen appeared in my flat unannounced. It turned out that she had wangled a large advance out of an American publisher and wanted to come back to England to write.

My trance-like state of mind made that first meeting strange. But, as I began to surface, the awkwardness gradually gave way to relief and soon we got on better. It seemed almost preferable that she knew only a little about what had happened.

By that Christmas we had moved out together to a tiny cottage in Suffolk. The east coast climate was sharp and bracing and gradually it began to shear away some of my remaining neuroses. Occasionally I got letters from writers researching the Weston murders which had now entered that limbo of half-unsolved crimes. Occultism, necrophilia, transsexuality; their approaches were in the usual line of halfbaked theorising. Often I didn't even feel like replying.

152

In the spring which followed, I learned that my sexology book had at last been confirmed for a major autumn launch. And walking through the sloping field to the pub for an impromptu celebration, I felt like someone who has dreamed a terrible nightmare about a shipwreck, and woken to find himself in a fine land-locked garden surrounded by flowers and green trees.

But was there, ever so far away, the sound of breakers somewhere?

Chapter Two

Two years later, when I was visiting London, the sea-wall broke.

It was complete chance. Weston and everything that had surrounded it were distant and displeasing memories. Almost as if they had happened to somebody else. Communications between the provinces and London were getting more difficult anyway. I sometimes used the Mini in London but always travelled to Suffolk by bus because only buses and taxis had easy access to long distance petrol. Once, when John had referred to the Weston affair obliquely, it took me a long time to grasp what he was talking about. The burial was a little too deep.

All that summer I had been preoccupied with some work on sexuality and spiritualism in the nineteenth century. I made frequent visits to the Library of Psychical Research near the French Lycée in South Kensington where I pored over dustry books from the period. One sunny Friday afternoon around noon I emerged from the little reading room to eat. I was already looking forward to going back to the country for the weekend.

As usual, in the middle of the day, the south side of Harrington Road was milling with French students and shoppers. Many of them were clustered around the latest in a long line of little patisseries, selling coffee and cream cakes. I thought of Paris.

It would never have happened if the mental association had not made me wonder if there was still a hotel on the other side of the road catering to French tourists.

I turned idly to look for it, and my view was blocked by a taxi, moving in the opposite direction. The nearest occupant was invisible because she had her back to me. All I could see was a fur-coat. But the other was leaning forward in what looked like earnest conversation: lips parted, eyes narrowed.

The anguish that expression invoked in me was so crushing that I must actually have cried out. The two people ahead of me stared round in surprise. All the intentions and desires with which I had woken that morning were obliterated. My throat felt like sand-paper, my legs swayed. Turning back with difficulty I could see the taxi signalling right at some traffic-lights along the street.

Without even a sense of decision I walked off the pavement straight into the path of an oncoming Harrods van. It swerved to one side narrowly missing me in a screaming skid. There was a noise of horns and shouts but I weaved on across the road and managed to get to my car.

By the time I pulled into the stream of traffic, the taxi had disappeared. It was only as I waited at the lights that I noticed my eyes were filled with tears.

By the time I finally took the corner, after some suicidal diagonal overtaking, I could just make out what I thought was the taxi, turning left into Kensington High Street. The lights must have slowed it up because halfway along the High Street, it was only a few cars in front and I was sure it was the same one.

We passed Shepherds Bush roundabout and the cab signalled left off the Goldhawk Road to turn into a residential street. I slowed down.

It was fortunate I did, because the taxi stopped almost immediately, outside a brightly painted two storey terrace house. I was able to halt on the corner.

Two women got out. It was not possible to see them properly but one was thin with a crumpled coat of what might have been suede, and the other looked bigger and older. She was dressed in the fur and she paid the cab. I watched them climbing the steps of the house and disappear inside as the taxi drove away.

After about five minutes, I got out and sauntered up the road to take a closer look. It was obvious the house was divided into flats. I walked up the steps and examined the names on the plate: Jones, Preston, Langport and Silver.

None of them meant anything. Pushing open the door, I found myself inside a gloomy hallway that smelled of frying bacon. There were flats on either side of a large central staircase. The building had been a medium-sized private residence before it was converted.

I went up and rang the Jones bell on the left-hand side. After a moment a big middle-aged black woman in trousers and blouse opened the door, with a little girl in pigtails wandering vaguely behind her.

'I'm looking for Miss . . . Daniels.' The name came out a little shakily. 'But I'm not quite sure of the flat number.'

'Not here,' the woman shrugged. 'There's two ladies above us for the summer,' she glanced upwards, 'but they may've gone already. Don't think it was a Daniels. Do you know?' she turned to her little daughter who was sucking a lollipop and clutching vaguely at her mother's trouser-leg. The little girl shook her head without much interest.

I thanked her and walked upstairs. The corresponding door above, marked Langport, was slightly smarter, painted white with a bright metal knocker in the shape of a horn. I rapped on it loudly.

For a long time nothing happened. Just as I was wondering whether to try again, a middle-aged woman opened it. She was in her mid-50s, I guessed, with lined but powerful features and intelligent grey eyes. The well-cut navy blue suit was not new but it had once been expensive. Behind her on a peg I could see a fur-coat. And behind that there were packing cases.

I smiled at her politely. 'I'm so sorry to bother you,' I said earnestly. 'I'm looking for someone. A Miss Daniels.'

Was I imagining an almost imperceptible reaction as I said the name? If there was one, she recovered smartly.

'Sorry you must have the wrong address.' Her voice was deep and cultivated. 'There's no-one here but me and as you see I'm in the process of moving out. Perhaps one of the other flats. . . .'

The door was closed before I could even thank her. In itself that wasn't suspicious. I had been staring into the flat with all the curiosity of a professional burglar.

I went back to the car and waited.

Finally, after an hour and a half of boredom and frustration, I resolved to give it another twenty minutes.

Then another five just for luck. It was beginning to get cold.

After five had stretched to twenty-five I gave up. There was a lot to do, it was insane to let a small thing like this break my routine. I was almost certainly mistaken anyway. I put out my hand to the ignition.

To my surprise it refused to turn. Or rather I refused to turn it. It was an odd feeling. The rational me wasn't any more in control than it had been since I left South Kensington. I knew then I was going to sit there until the person I had seen came out of that house.

As darkness fell I became increasingly cold and uncomfortable. Half a dozen people went into the house and two men came out but there were no other developments. I wanted to go to the toilet and I was hungry. I revved the motor to get some heat into the car, but I was unable to take my eyes off those steps. Hours passed.

At about eleven-thirty something happened. The woman in the fur-coat re-emerged. She was alone and she walked off down the road in the other direction. There was still a light in the top-left apartment.

After she was out of sight, I got out of the car and made my way back towards the flats. Most of the other windows were dark.

Inside, the hall was unlit but I found a white time-switch by the door. In the dim light of a single bulb, I walked up the flight of stairs with my heart bumping and rapped on the horn-knocker.

The time-switch clicked off, leaving me in the darkness as the knock echoed down the hall.

I stood there immobile. Like you do after a really awful nightmare, dreading that something will creep out into reality from the film in your head.

The door opened slowly and she was standing in the shadows.

Chapter Three

There is still no terror quite so pure as the terror that you are hallucinating, that your mind has lost any kind of plausible relation to reality. Even the post-LSD generation retains it.

I must have closed my eyes because, when I opened them again, Johanna was still standing there and looking at me. We both looked.

'Did the resurrection go well?' I said with self-conscious anger as if I was talking to myself in someone else's presence. 'You look more together than in the photos.'

She gave a sharp intake of breath but she didn't answer. I went forward into the room. It was large and completely empty apart from a small suitcase and an electric fire. Johanna shut the door, and, still leaning against it, she turned back to face me.

'I don't see why you had to get involved,' she said. Her voice sounded ghostly, with a slight intonation that was unfamiliar. Later I realised it was American.

I shrugged. 'Personal interest.'

She turned away towards the small two bar electric radiator, squatting down by it to warm her hands. There were a couple of opened bottles beside her – vodka and milk – and she reached out for them. It was cold in the room.

'Tomorrow's breakfast. Would you like some?'

I sat down on the other side of the fire. 'Hard or soft?' I asked.

She poured some vodka into a tumbler and tipped a little splash of milk on top. It curdled out like a tiny white jellyfish. 'Not soft.'

I didn't take any. I knew that the only way I could cope was to hold onto the anger.

I tried to scrutinise her appearance as objectively as I could. The hair was shorter and the complexion paler. A sharp contrast between the spiky cut and the pallor of her

158

skin. The nose was still freckled. In those bare surroundings, the crumpled and slightly grubby chic of the coat made her look strange and almost comic, like a routed dreamer.

'Why aren't you dead?' It was as blunt as I felt but she didn't answer.

'Angela went on ahead after I decided not to avoid you,' she said clumsily.

'Who's Angela?'

She gulped her vodka with milk. 'In the fur. I may not know her too long.' Then, as if realising she wasn't making much sense she looked up at me: 'Look, I want you to know about it. That's why I didn't run away when you turned up today. We're only back here for a few weeks. Angie rescued me from something in New York, and I've been living with her since. I don't know how long it'll last.'

She must have caught my thought. 'It's not a money thing,' she said. And then for the first time her face took on a trace of a smile: 'I've been doing pretty well without that kind of reality lately.'

'Whose body was it?' I asked quietly. Of course I knew now but I wanted to keep asking concrete questions.

'I don't know,' she said. It sounded true.

Another pause. I began to wonder if she really intended to tell me anything. The empty room seemed to be mirroring the conversation. There wasn't even a rug to cover the parquet floor. It was a peculiarly painful setting. To keep from looking at her face, I examined the plain brown suitcase by the door, and the blue window curtains.

'It wasn't too clear from those stories in the papers,' she said finally, 'if you knew about what was happening in Weston.'

As neutrally as I could I outlined some of my discoveries; and what Paines had told me, though I left out his death. She listened attentively but it was obvious I was conveying nothing new. She seemed much more interested when I described what had happened on that Christmas night when I first drove to the town.

'They were scared by then,' she interrupted at one point. 'That was why it was so dangerous.'

After I had finished I sat there waiting for her to tell me how she got involved.

'Jane Triar,' she said at last. She spoke flatly but it was as

159

if the introduction of that name, the name of the first murder victim, would alter our conversation irrevocably. 'She had gone through . . . something with her father.' Her voice shook and she leaned forward to pour another vodka and milk, drinking it more slowly this time, starting to unwind. 'When we moved in together she would still wake up screaming even though she hadn't seen him for four years. She'd been brought up in Weston but her parents moved away when she was still quite young.'

Her hand twisted snake-like around the glass as she stared into the fire. 'You see America had been pretty bad for me after Mum died. When I got back here I didn't know anyone until I met Jane in some stupid drama evening class in Manchester. After that, we lived a bit like hermits. I had money, we didn't need work. Or men. We were happy.'

Outside a single car accelerated past the house and braked sharply at the junction with Goldhawk Road. A child began crying in the flat below and I remembered the little girl in the afternoon with the lollipop. But Johanna seemed oblivious to these externals.

'The thing began because Jane had been friendly with this guy from the town. She had a thing about really young guys. You know sixteen, seventeen. She met Hamish in London when he'd run away from home. It turned out he was from Weston. But he went back and stopped writing, and when she tried to visit him the parents wouldn't let her. We were in the town trying to find out more and we met one of Jane's old classmates on her way back from the pregnancy clinic. A fat red-faced little girl. Most of what she told us was hair-raising. She didn't even know who the father was but it was one of her family. We knew then that the whole place was going like that. Ever since the curfews.

'Then one night we were sitting in our flat in Manchester talking about it when we got an obscene phone call. Pure chance – the phone wasn't even in our name. Jane was a bit stoned, and she came on really sexy and aggressive, which terrified him. And that was the beginning of the whole idea.

'How you could smash the pattern in Weston by objecti-fying sex again. By fantasy. It started like a secret game we had. Just fooling around. Then it became something more – a kind of idiot mission. We changed flats. Clothes, characters, names, even dialogue. It was addictive. The families had the

160

whole place on its knees, we wanted to hit them. To begin with we did. There were ripples.'

'How often did you go there?'

'Rarely. We intended to create as much mystery as possible. We could make costume changes in the old pub. For the clients we used the car. I checked into the hotel at the very beginning but that was difficult.' I thought of the shaky signature in the register. Johanna drank some more. She must have been quite drunk by now but it hardly showed.

'Even the physical side didn't bother us because it didn't bother the parts we were playing. We had a joke about it. That all you needed was Vaseline and a strong personality.'

She repeated the words with a strange mixture of passion and derision. 'Shit we were so sickeningly romantic looking back on it. We'd seen *Klute* too many times.'

Then I realised why her alias had been so familiar. Bree Daniels. It was the name of the crusading prostitute played by Jane Fonda in the film *Klute*. The prostitute-as-liberator.

'What about travelling salesmen?' I don't think I even meant to say it aloud.

But she just grinned bitterly: 'Yes. After all, pour encourager les autres. There had to be some sacrifices.'

Silence. 'One of them saved my life as it happens,' she added.

She leaned closer to the radiator, one hand pulling at a lock of hair.

'Unintentionally . . . It was the night Jane got hit. Just after she left, a policeman I'd never seen came into the bar, and muttered something about seeing how many of them we could take on later. But the salesman had been feeding me triples on the sly and I passed out in his room.'

Her lips curled up in revulsion. 'He must have mauled me most of the night. By the time I came round it was morning and the news about Jane was on the radio. Even in that state I saw how blind we'd both been. The police had been watching us. It was a trap. They knew.

'I managed to convince the salesman we should leave town together.'

'But couldn't they trace you?'

'They got close. It was an awful time.' She looked up at me and smiled. 'I wasn't safe until Johanna let rip with her

161

most prominent instinct. Her only positive trait as far as I'm concerned.'

Something about the way she said it made me shiver: 'Which was?'

'Self-destruction.' she said flatly. 'Don't you remember?'

My mind raced back to that last overdose phone-call so many years ago, the stuttering slurred voice. 'But I don't get the. . .?'

'By planting the clothes,' she said. 'Or rather by paying someone to plant them. The only moment of genius Johanna ever had. The man I used thought it was just a drugs drop with coke in the lining of each item. He does plenty.'

'But why?'

'Because I had realised by then,' she said plainly 'that it was over and I wanted them to think I was dead. Paines got an anonymous note with some identification saying I was dead. What they could never know was that by doing it that way they were actually doing me an impossible favour. Johanna had always wanted to destroy herself. Now she did it. It was like. . .' she struggled to express it '. . .like new skin.'

'As Bree Daniels?'

'As anyone I wanted.'

The flat was very silent. It was a kind of collusion. They may not have believed the note but they could be pretty sure Johanna was not going to come forward. And Marie presented a very convenient stand-in corpse. I felt sick. 'You didn't want to get back at them.' It was hardly even a question.

'I thought about it. They killed someone I love. Jane. But they also killed someone I hate. Johanna. After a time, the two cancel each other out.'

Johanna, the guerilla psyche.

'So aren't you breaking your own rules by talking to me?'

She grinned amicably: 'You're not important to them now any more than I am. In their language, I'm the nation's favourite ripped whore and you're the favourite crank. The fact that neither of us are what we seem has nothing to do with it.'

'But what about the people they did kill?' I said.

Johanna shrugged: 'So what about them?'

That was her most cold, in jarring contrast to her tone a moment earlier. And yet it wasn't even cold. It was just drunkenly self-centred and cynical. But it hit hard.

162

'Maybe you should have been the corpse after all,' I said.
'Because if it hadn't been for Weatherspoon and your happy
little stand-in Marie, it would have been you or me or anyone.' I paused, hoping the words would sink in. 'But then
Jane's carving ceremony doesn't seem to have bothered you
much either.'

Johanna looked straight at me. 'I've thought about it,' she
said eventually, in a flat monotone. 'You and Weatherspoon.
Male explorers. Jane and I were conning ourselves too but
not in that patronising way. OK, we didn't know it was a
conspiracy, but it wouldn't have surprised us much if we had.
We'd have just avoided it. You came right to its rescue, not
ours; you even delivered another victim at the same time.'

She got up then, hugging her shoulders, and went over to
the window.

'You see,' she murmured. 'What you'll never understand
is that some things are a lot more important than watching
men fuck each other around.'

I tried to answer but couldn't.

Then she turned back to me and I was ten years ago,
running up a flight of dirty stairs, knowing she was at the top.

Perhaps she caught the memory: 'I'm not as far away as
you're thinking,' she said, coming towards me. 'It's just a
different place. I've had a chance to move and I've moved.'
She paused. 'But I'm not going back.'

'So why did you let me come?' I asked. It wasn't a devious
question. I felt genuinely baffled, like a small boy at the North
Pole addressing Santa Claus.

'Because you saw me,' she said, 'I wanted you to know.
Also to say goodbye properly.'

She sat down again and put out a hand. I took it. It was
a cold Martian hand.

Last try.

'Don't you see,' I pleaded, 'that if I produce you the whole
conspiracy falls? We can get them.'

'I don't think you even skimmed the surface,' she said.
'And there are far more of them than there are of us. After
all, I don't even exist, remember?'

The knocking at the door was sudden and violent. I jumped
an inch and the nails dug into my palms. 'Taxi,' a voice
called. Johanna went straight over.

She opened the door and disappeared. I sat back down by

163

the fire, registering the large vodka bottle. About two thirds of it had been drunk, and on an impulse I picked it up and drained enough of what was left.

I was mentally exhausted and I hadn't eaten in 24 hours so the effects were instant. I felt limp and my eyes watered, but the horrible sharpness of that room began to blur.

'I'll be just a few minutes,' I heard her saying. 'If you wait down there it won't take too long.'

She shut the door and walked out of the blur to sit beside me. Grinning, her head to one side.

'No I still don't know the best way to do this,' she said finally. ' I can be Bree, if that's how we should go out.'

The remark, which was also an invitation, hung there a long time, like a bracket. After all this, Johanna was an unbelievable two feet away from me. She was flushed, there were lines under her eyes, and I could smell a faint odour of sweat and deodorant. Yet she might have been at the foot of the Andes. The mystery was as intense as ever.

It wasn't the mundane mystery of conspiracy. Not the mechanical determination of who shot who and why. But the mystery that will lead a child to dread it is the only living player in a monstrous puppet theatre designed by God.

Sex always fields the best clues. But even in a sexual relationship the certainty that there is anyone else there can vanish overnight, or slide away with agonising imperceptible slowness, like a long summer afternoon.

As the moment hung on, it seemed to me suddenly in my drunkenness that there is a strict celestial rule about that. In every human relationship, the last page, the solution or the resolution, is always torn out. You never get to know who did it. Jo and I were examining the chilling whiteness of that page now. Occasionally we might spot a few words scrawled across it. But they were illegible anyway. The graffiti that would return to haunt us some other time or place. Later, when we came to write our own impossibly conflicting versions.

I could never fully disentangle the mixture of motives in what happened next; on my side there was little lust, some fear, a futile wish to try and exorcise the mystery. And also a sort of inflamed terror because she was able to offer sex as a way of saying goodbye, with the taxi-driver waiting downstairs. The most vivid memory is how much I wanted her to take the coat off.

She didn't come. In fact, she had to use some of the milk to make it easier in the beginning. Her body felt small and tight like a little girl. I remember my right hand was on the side of her head, touching the hair and she was looking up.

Afterwards I lay staring down at the boards, with the phrase about Vaseline going round and round in my head.

I watched blankly while she was dressed. She put on a red jersey and a black skirt, adjusting her hair. She looked intent.

Did I really pass out, or was that part of an elaborate unconscious game to avoid the last look? When my brain cleared there was only a long white landscape with pockmarks and craters, stretching away into nothing.

It was milk. I was lying in a pool of it on the floor of an empty room.

Every time Armitage pressed the lift button, he could hear the same impotent clanking from somewhere above him. Either someone had got the door jammed or it was broken again. He steeled himself for the four flights of stairs, trying to console his tired muscles with the thought that it was just as well June and he had sweated blood to find their bungalow. They couldn't have stuck it in one of Weston's tower-blocks. Although up to now he had heard surprisingly few complaints from the residents. You never even saw much graffiti.

On the fourth landing he was irritated to find that the lift-door had been obstructed by an ancient rusted roller-skate. He kicked it out of the way and the doors banged smartly shut. Kids. He was in a bad enough temper already. During his first two years in personnel at the works he'd only had to make one home visit, and now this was the tenth this month. Perhaps the British disease was catching on here as it had everywhere else. But so far he had to admit his random checks had turned up only genuine accidents and illness. No sign at all of the creeping absenteeism his employers feared.

The teenage girl who opened the door took a long time understanding who he was. Her mother was out shopping and she seemed a bit vague. But at last she led him through the tiny cluttered flat to a small overheated room at the back, where her father was lying miserably in hideous bright pyjamas like a beached whale. Apparently he had fractured his leg on the stairs the previous day while playing with his children and no-one had got around to ringing up. There was a thick bulge of plaster under the blanket.

As he talked, Armitage's eyes ran discreetly over the room. But even without the medical certificate there would have been no doubt. The smell of pain and discomfort was much too palpable to be feigned. Patches of sweat soaked the man's pyjamas and he breathed heavily. Armitage felt a flash of pity, but it was accompanied by the guilty knowledge that he was already in a slightly better temper. Work would be pleased to hear it was just another accident.

His guilt and satisfaction made him generous and on his way out he slipped a few pounds to the girl with instructions to buy her dad something to cheer him up. The lift was no longer there. This time he could hear nothing at all when he pressed the button. Perhaps someone was using it higher up.

Walking back down the stairs, Armitage suddenly recalled with a shock that this was about the sixth accident in as many weeks. Fortunately they were all domestic but why in hell should the workforce have chosen this winter to start tripping over? Maybe it was the cold

166

weather; he'd better make some enquiries about the adequacy of these lifts.

Some children were on the second landing playing in a tight little group. He knew they must belong to the sick man's household and tried to talk to them but they stared back at him monosyllabically without much interest.

Only one small boy sucking a lolly seemed more curious than the others and he began to follow a little way behind on the stairs. He came as far as the ground floor landing and then stopped. As if the front door was a sign he should go no further.

Armitage walked hurriedly across the empty car-park. It was already later and darker than he expected. Standing beside his bicycle, he quickly filled in the basic visit-form and thrust it into the brief-case on the holder, only just remembering to switch on the dynamo light. As he came abreast of the building on the road, he was amused to see that the kids were outside it now. They were playing red indians or something. Dancing round and round the tower-block.